Twin Sister Swap

One month to change their lives!

Identical twin sisters Rowan and Willow may be
alike in looks, but both lead very different lives.
Dress designer Rowan prefers the anonymity of the
Cornish coast while supermodel Willow belongs in
the upper echelons of the New York socialite scene.
Yet when Willow finds herself needing to hide from
the world for a while, she knows there is only
one person who can step into her shoes and
rescue her—temporarily...

But pulling off their twin swap and trading lives
without a hitch is more of a challenge than
they anticipated...especially when faced
with unexpected romance...!

See what happens when reclusive Rowan steps out
of her comfort zone and into the Big Apple and
the arms of tycoon Eli while pretending to be
her sister in *Cinderella in the Spotlight*.

And in *Socialite's Nine-Month Secret*, after finding
out she's pregnant, Willow knows she needs some
anonymity for a while to reassess her future—alone.
Until she meets the man next door and suddenly
her new plan is thrown into delicious chaos!

Both available now!

T0015166

Dear Reader,

I've had so much fun writing this life-swap duet. While the first book was very much about stepping out of your comfort zone in a big way, Willow and Gwyn's story was always going to be more about hiding away. But while both of them are trying to hide from their problems and pasts in the wider world, it turns out that you can't hide from the reality living inside you—quite literally in Willow's case!

I hope you enjoy Willow's journey of discovery as she falls in love with the seaside village of Rumbelow—and a certain handsome musician neighbor. And maybe you will a little bit, too...

Love and confetti,

Sophie x

Socialite's
Nine-Month Secret

─────

Sophie Pembroke

HARLEQUIN®

Romance™

Recycling programs
for this product may
not exist in your area.

ISBN-13: 978-1-335-59668-0

Socialite's Nine-Month Secret

Copyright © 2024 by Sophie Pembroke

For questions and comments about the quality of this book,
please contact us at CustomerService@Harlequin.com.

TM and ® are trademarks of Harlequin Enterprises ULC.

Harlequin Enterprises ULC
22 Adelaide St. West, 41st Floor
Toronto, Ontario M5H 4E3, Canada
www.Harlequin.com

Printed in U.S.A.

Sophie Pembroke has been dreaming, reading and writing romance ever since she read her first Harlequin novel as part of her English literature degree at Lancaster University, so getting to write romantic fiction for a living really is a dream come true! Born in Abu Dhabi, Sophie grew up in Wales and now lives in a little Hertfordshire market town with her scientist husband, her incredibly imaginative and creative daughter, and her adventurous, adorable little boy. In Sophie's world, happy *is* forever after, everything stops for tea and there's always time for one more page...

Books by Sophie Pembroke

Harlequin Romance

Dream Destinations
Their Icelandic Marriage Reunion
Baby Surprise in Costa Rica

The Heirs of Wishcliffe
Vegas Wedding to Forever
Their Second Chance Miracle
Baby on the Rebel Heir's Doorstep

Twin Sister Swap
Cinderella in the Spotlight

The Princess and the Rebel Billionaire
Best Man with Benefits

Visit the Author Profile page
at Harlequin.com for more titles.

For anyone who feels the need to hide away from the world for a little while. I know you'll come out fighting when you're ready.

Praise for
Sophie Pembroke

CHAPTER ONE

AFTER A LONG FLIGHT, a sleepless night in an airport hotel and too many hours in the town car she'd hired to drive her from London to Cornwall, the sight of the first sign for the village of Rumbelow sent relief flooding through Willow's tense body.

She'd made it—near enough, anyway. And, as far as she could tell from social media, without being spotted, which was the most important thing.

Nobody would be looking for supermodel and socialite Willow Harper in Cornwall, when she was supposed to be in New York. What possible reason could she have to go there?

Even those who remembered the early days of her career, when she'd modelled with her twin sister, didn't know where Rowan had fled to when she'd disappeared six years ago. The family had no link to Cornwall, despite hailing from London originally, and Rowan had been *very* circumspect regarding her where-abouts ever since. Willow suspected she was the only person from their old life who knew where she was at all.

And even she hadn't visited, or seen Rowan, in those six years.

Until now.

Because now she needed her help.

The car and its silent driver took the last curve in the road and the small harbour of Rumbelow came into view, the sea glisten-ing in the early spring sunlight. Tiny fishing boats bobbed out on the waves—so different from the mega yachts and sailing club boats she'd grown used to in her society circles in the States.

They drove along the edge of the village, the long black car slowing almost to a stop to make the tight corners safely, and Wil-low peered out of the tinted windows at the quaintly painted cottages and the cobblestone streets that led away from the road and into the village centre.

It was a pretty enough hiding spot, she had to allow that—for Rowan, and for her.

Rowan's cottage, it seemed, was on the out-skirts of the village. They drove around the out-side to the other side of the harbour, where the glass and steel outline of what appeared to be an old lifeboat station that someone had converted into living accommodation gleamed in the distance above the waves. Before that, though, was a small stone cottage with a thatched roof, looking down on the beach below, its sand covered in seaweed and stones, and over at the cliffs beyond, now the neat harbour had given way to more natural coastline.

The driver drew the car to a halt and got out in silence, the same way he'd undertaken the entire journey. She heard the trunk of the car open and assumed he was getting out her suitcase. She waited and, soon enough, he opened the door for her and she climbed out.

It was the air that hit her first: salty and tangy and fresh as a steady breeze beat against her skin and tried to mess up her hair. There was no reason for it to feel so different from the coast in the States, really, but it did. If she closed her eyes, she could be back at the seaside with her grandparents, Rowan paddling beside her, waiting for salty chips and sweet, sticky ice cream.

Before her grandparents died. And before that scout told their mother how much money they could make her.

Willow swallowed and shook the thought

away. She had nothing to complain about. Her whole world had changed that moment—and look how far it had taken her. She had fame, riches, a life others would kill for.

Right now, though, she also had a secret.

The driver was looking dubiously at Rowan's little stone cottage. Willow supposed she couldn't blame him; it did look a little like it might crumble into the sea at any moment.

'Do you have the keys, miss?' he asked, his voice a little creaky. 'I can take your bags in for you.'

'Uh, actually, I'm just going to wait here for my sister.' Along the cliff path, she could see a figure approaching, perhaps from that lifeboat station, since it seemed the only house further out of the village than Rowan's. 'You can just leave my bags here, it's fine.'

The driver frowned. 'Are you absolutely sure?'

'Very.' Willow swallowed down her irritation and forced a smile. She needed him to go, and fast, before Rowan's neighbour got any closer and started asking questions. She fumbled in her bag for a tip, and thrust a few notes into his hand. 'Thank you for the drive. Please, you should get going. It's a long way back to London.'

He gave her one more sceptical look, then took the money and got back into the car, reversing slowly into a side path to enable himself to turn around without driving off the cliff. The car disappeared towards the town before Rowan's neighbour reached her front gate, and Willow let out a small sigh of relief. She settled on sitting on top of her suitcase while she waited for her sister, her eyes tracking the neighbour as they jogged closer.

He. Definitely a he. With strong muscled legs under his running shorts and a black T-shirt already clinging to his torso. His dark hair hung long enough for him to shake it out of his eyes as he ran, and he was moving at an impressive pace. Willow ran, for fitness, stress relief and because it looked good in paparazzi photos, but she never went fast enough that she ended up unpleasantly red-faced and sweaty in those photos. She saved that sort of effort for the private gym in her Manhattan building.

But this guy was moving fast and *still* looked good. She was almost jealous.

She jerked her gaze away as he approached the gate and, standing quickly, dropped her tan leather jacket over her bags in the hope he wouldn't notice them, pushing them slightly behind the overgrown shrubbery of Rowan's front garden.

'Morning!' he called as he reached the edge of the fence marking her property.

'Uh, yeah,' she said back, somewhat taken by surprise. 'Morning.'

In New York, locals and tourists barely acknowledged other people with a nod, let alone a verbal greeting.

You're not in New York any more, Willow.

For all she knew, Rowan was best friends with her neighbour round the harbour. Maybe they had coffee together every morning. Maybe they were *more* than friends.

In which case, her sister had definitely been holding out on her during their calls, and she was in for a grilling.

The guy slowed to a stop at the gate, one hand on the fence as he looked at her, a small frown line between his eyebrows. 'You lock yourself out or something? I can run back and get my spare key if you need it.'

He had a spare key. Okay, so friends, then.

He also thought she was Rowan, even if the frown suggested he sensed something was amiss.

'Oh, no, I'm fine, thanks. Just…enjoying the morning.'

'Not contemplating joining me for a run at last?' The teasing tone of his voice hinted that this was something he suggested often.

Willow shook her head. 'I don't think I'm dressed for it.'

'No.' And now that frown was back, as he looked her up and down. 'Big plans today? You're looking very…smart.'

She glanced down at herself in case she'd suddenly changed into a ballgown or something. Nope, same wide-leg nude trousers and black sweater, with her chestnut leather boots. It was warm enough that she'd even taken her tan leather jacket off for now.

'No, just…a normal day. Perfectly normal.'

Oh, yeah, that sounded convincing.

And from the way the guy's eyebrows rose, he wasn't convinced either.

Gwyn looked at his neighbour with what he could only think of as amused suspicion.

He and Rowan weren't exactly close friends, but they *were* neighbours, the two furthest out dwellings in the village, and so they'd got to know each other a little. They had spare keys to each other's houses, checked with each other on bin days and WhatsApped snippets from the local village Facebook group for their mutual entertainment.

And he jogged past her cottage every morning and more often than not spotted her on her way in or back from the village centre, or working in her garden, or just pottering about inside the cottage. Sometimes she'd wave. Sometimes he'd invite her to join him and she'd laugh and shake her head. Sometimes he'd stop for a chat, especially if he was on his way back and kind of already done and needing a break before the last burst up the hill and round the harbour to his house.

But never, in all the years they'd been doing this, had he ever seen Rowan in full makeup, her hair brushed and her shoes shined at this time in the morning. Or ever. He'd never seen her wearing clothes so plain and colourless either.

And he'd never seen her hiding a suitcase under her coat, for that matter.

Was she going somewhere and didn't want him—or, by extension, probably the rest of the village—to know about it?

Rumbelow was a small place. And as much as the locals let newcomers live their own lives without asking too many questions, that didn't mean they weren't watching. Or talking about them behind their backs.

Gwyn wasn't a newcomer, exactly—although he suspected Rowan thought he was. After all, he'd bought the most obvious, expensive, fancy modern renovation place in the whole village when he'd moved back from London. That wasn't *why* he'd bought it, of course—he'd bought it because it was the furthest out of Rumbelow he could be while still being in the village, and because it only had one real neighbour, and because he liked looking out over the sea from the giant glass windows that used to be the doors to the lifeboat shed.

Rowan, as far as he knew, didn't know that Gwyn's family had been in the village for generations, or that his sister and nephew still lived there. She didn't know he'd grown up there, moved away, then come home when everything had fallen apart.

But then he suspected Rowan still thought that nobody in town had clocked that she used to be a kind of famous model, when obviously they had, almost immediately. They were just too polite around here to make a big deal of it, since she so obviously didn't want a big deal being made.

None of which explained why she was sitting there with a suitcase, looking like she was about to head up to London for some big fashion shoot. Maybe she was. Maybe that was what she was hiding—or hoping he wouldn't notice.

Well, if she wanted to keep her secrets, he'd let her. After all, he had no interest in sharing his own.

So he gave her a last smile and said, 'Okay, well, enjoy your day.' Then he pushed off again and began the easy run down the hill back into the village, planning to stop in at his sister's to see if she had any coffee on the go, and maybe some of those cinnamon rolls she made...

Which was when he spotted Rowan walking up the hill towards him, wearing the bright turquoise and pink maxi skirt he often saw her in, her hair in its usual bun on the top of her head and a straw shopping bag swinging at her side as she smiled and waved.

He blinked, almost stumbled and then kept going.

Other people's secrets were none of his business. And neither were their problems.

Although he had to admit he was curious as to what supermodel Willow Harper was doing pretending to be her own sister, right here in Rumbelow.

* * *

Willow braced herself as she saw her sister appear around the corner, looking as bright and cheerful as she always did on their video calls these days—a sort of relaxed contentment that Willow couldn't remember seeing in person since they were kids.

It was real, that contentment, she was sure. But she always felt there was just a hint of something missing underneath it too. A feeling that Rowan had settled for contentment rather than reaching for happiness.

Willow stifled a snort. Who was she to talk about happiness as something to be actively pursued? Hadn't she spent the last few years settling for image—style over substance—in all areas of her life?

Not any more, though. I can't do that any longer.

And maybe her new resolution to do better could help her sister find the life she was meant to be living too. Even if she had doubts at how effective her plan would be at *really* fixing everything that was wrong in her own life.

I just need time. Space. To breathe and think and figure things out.

Rowan was the only person in the world that Willow could rely on to give it to her.

She knew the moment that her twin spotted her. It was obvious in the way her easy gait faltered, and her shoulders stiffened even as her face slackened.

Maybe she should have called ahead, told her she was coming. Or emailed, even. Except…she was never sure how secure those things were. All it would take was one journalist listening in or hacking her email and her secret would be out.

Because Rowan was going to have questions—a lot of questions. Questions Willow needed to answer in person, without being overheard, if she wanted to keep her secrets.

Suddenly Rowan shook her head and hurried towards the gate, fumbling for her keys even as she stepped onto the path.

'What are you *doing* here?' Her whisper was harsh, unwelcoming, as she fiddled with the lock until the door fell open. 'Come on, come in. Before someone sees you.'

Willow did as she was told, following her sister into the tiny, dark cottage. Not quite the homecoming she'd been hoping for, but that probably served her right for showing up with no notice.

'How long have you been here?' The door slammed behind them.

Willow raised her eyebrows. 'In England or on your doorstep?'

'Both.'

Willow placed her large tote bag on the floor beside the telephone table and frowned at the old-fashioned rotary dial phone that sat there. How ridiculously impractical. And convenient for her, actually.

'I arrived in England last night,' she said, straightening up again. 'I stayed at a hotel near Heathrow, then got a car to bring me down here this morning. I'd been standing on your doorstep for about ten minutes when you arrived. I did try to call, but...'

She gave the rotary dial phone another dubious look to back up her little white lie.

'Cell signal can be unreliable here.' Rowan carried her own tatty straw bag down the darkened hall into a decidedly brighter kitchen at the back of the cottage. It looked out over a higgledy-piggledy garden that looked like someone—presumably Rowan—might have been trying to grow vegetables.

This really was another world.

Rowan emptied her bag out onto the battered kitchen table. 'Croissant?'

The morning sickness had mostly passed now, which she took to mean she was probably past twelve weeks, since that was when all the websites she'd read in secret said it would. But mornings had never been Willow's favourite time to eat, and after a long flight and a lengthy car journey her stomach turned at the idea of the flaky pastry. She shook her head and Rowan bit into one with a shrug.

Willow looked away, taking in the kitchen, with its mismatched sage and lavender chairs that matched the pots of lavender growing outside the window. It was a sunny, happy place. It suited Rowan.

Willow had never felt more out of place in her life.

Still, when her sister motioned for her to sit, she did. And then she got down to why she was there.

'I need your help.'

Rowan reached for another croissant. 'That doesn't sound good.'

Willow knew why. This wasn't the way things went. Willow didn't come to Rowan for help; it had always, always been the other way around, ever since they were kids.

Willow had been the strong, capable one. Rowan the one who needed protecting, looking out for.

When Rowan had needed to leave, Willow had been the one to get her out—and the one to stay behind and face the wrath of their mother, and all those contracts Rowan had walked out on.

Rowan hid, Willow stayed and faced the music.

But this time…this time it needed to be the other way round. It was time for Willow to call in that favour.

'What do you need?' Rowan asked cautiously.

Willow glanced towards the kettle. 'I think we might need tea for this.' She would have preferred coffee, but apparently tea was better right now. She'd been trying to limit herself to just one strong coffee in the mornings, and she'd already had that on the way from the airport.

She waited until her sister had got up to find mugs and tea leaves and an actual teapot, complete with knitted cosy, and poured the tea. Then she took a deep breath and said, 'I'm going to have a baby.'

'You're *pregnant*?' Rowan plonked one of the mugs of tea down in front of her, and Willow watched a few drops slosh onto the table top. 'How did that happen?'

'It certainly wasn't planned, I can tell you

that.' Willow sighed and reached for her mug, blowing slightly over the surface so steam snaked up towards the ceiling. The *plan,* such as it was, had been very, very different. If it had been *planned* she might have a better idea when exactly it had happened, but her cycle had never been regular enough for that. Still, that many pregnancy tests didn't lie.

'Who's the father? Does he know?' Rowan demanded.

'Ben, of course.' Willow frowned at her sister across the kitchen table. 'What did you think?'

'Sorry. I just...' Rowan trailed off. She'd never met Ben, Willow supposed. She wouldn't know. 'I guess I figured that if the father was your long-term boyfriend you'd be talking to him instead of me.'

That made Willow wince and look away towards the window. Talking to Ben was right at the bottom of her list of things she wanted to do right now.

How on earth was she going to explain her relationship with Ben to Rowan? Rowan believed in true love and authenticity and finding your person.

She wasn't going to understand what Willow had with Ben.

'Things with Ben and me…it's not what I'd call a stable relationship environment. Or anything a kid should be involved in.' Willow took care to keep her words flat, unemotional. But Rowan's expression told her she was reading plenty into them, all the same.

'Does he hurt you? Physically or emotionally? Because you do *not* have to go back to him—'

'It's not like that.' Willow sighed. 'He's… I mean, we're…'

'You're really convincing me here, Will.'

Willow huffed a laugh and looked down at her tea again. Fine. It was going to have to be the truth, then. However shameful it felt in the face of Rowan's fairy tale cottage by the sea life.

'I know. I'm sorry. It's just…the world thinks we're some fairy tale romance, right? The supermodel and the CEO, living our perfect glamorous life together, madly in love?'

'And it's not really like that?' Rowan asked softly.

It was, she supposed, in parts. They *were* a supermodel and a CEO, and their life was pretty glamorous, certainly from the outside.

It was just the *in love* part that tripped the whole thing up.

'You know, some days I'm not sure we even *like* each other,' Willow admitted. 'Right from the start…we were together because it was good for our images, our careers. We look good next to each other, and the papers like to talk about us a lot, and that was kind of what we both needed. We could fake the rest.'

Her mind flashed back to the night they'd met, at some party held by a mutual acquaintance. The way they'd sized each other up, figuring out what the other could offer them in a world where everything was a commodity or a status symbol. Even love.

'You *faked* being in love with your boyfriend?' Rowan made it sound like a bad rom com movie.

'Not…intentionally.' Willow sighed again. She'd known Rowan wasn't going to get it. She was barely sure that *she* understood how it had all happened.

But Rowan was obviously determined to try. 'Okay, tell me the whole story.'

CHAPTER TWO

THERE WAS NO sign of Rowan or the woman Gwyn assumed must be her sister when he jogged past the cottage towards home at the end of his run. That in itself was suspicious. Normally Rowan would be in the garden on a day like today; from the road, he could see all the way around the cottage into the back. But there was no sign of her, and the kitchen blinds had been tilted half closed too.

A clandestine visit, then.

Rowan had never mentioned her twin sister, but the identical part of their twin status was definitely no longer in doubt. If he hadn't seen the *real* Rowan just moments later, he'd have probably assumed she was just dressed up for a secret event and left it at that.

As it was, his mind kept ticking over the differences as he ran. He didn't know Rowan well enough to have been able to tell that the woman on the doorstep wasn't her—they were friends, but in a very loose, wave in the street sort of way. He wasn't even sure if *she* considered them friends.

But that was as friendly as Gwyn got these days. He didn't want to let new people in, and she didn't seem keen on the idea either, so that was fine.

Still, now he thought about it…

She'd held herself differently, maybe that was the big one. More…defensive? No. Assertive. As if she held the power here. Rowan never stood that way.

And he'd felt a sort of nervous tension coiled inside her as she spoke, but there was still a hint of something behind her eyes. A spark, as she looked him over.

He'd never felt *that* when talking about the latest bin collection shambles with Rowan.

Still, she'd obviously wanted him to believe she was her sister. Why? Why was she here at all, for that matter? She must need or want something from Rowan.

He wondered what.

He didn't spend *too* much time wondering though; other people's lives weren't his business—which meant they couldn't be his problem either. And that was the way he liked it.

But when he reached home he saw one of the

few people whose lives *were* his business—and often his problem—waiting for him.

Gwyn slowed to a halt on the steps down to the deck that surrounded this half of his ex-lifeboat station home, resting his hands on his thighs as he caught his breath. 'Sean. Everything okay?'

It wasn't that his nephew never came to see him unless there was something wrong, but… actually, yes, it was exactly that.

But Sean just shoved his hands deeper into the pockets of his jeans and nodded. 'Yeah, all good. I just…there was something I wanted to talk to you about.'

Oh, that was worse than there being a problem to solve. Sean wanted his *advice*. Didn't he know how bad Gwyn was at giving that?

He moved past Sean to unlock the side door and let them in. 'Have you spoken to your mother about it?'

Gwyn's sister, Abigail, was the best at knowing what to do and giving advice. Why Sean had decided to come to him instead was a mystery.

'Yeah, a bit.' Sean eyed him cautiously, still hovering in the doorway with his hands in his pockets. 'She said that you'd be the one to ask, except you wouldn't want to talk about it.'

Gwyn's shoulders tensed involuntarily. That

didn't bode well at all. Although, in fairness, there were a lot of things he didn't want to talk about.

'We're going to need coffee for this, I reckon,' he said, and moved towards the kitchen.

When he'd decided to move home to Rumbe-low—although *decided* was a bit strong, wasn't it? Given that he'd mostly stumbled back in a panic and crashed on his sister's sofa for the first six months. But when he'd decided to *stay*, and buy his own place, discovering that the old lifeboat station was up for sale had felt like a sign.

Now, standing in his kitchen, looking out at the waves as he pressed buttons on the coffee machine on autopilot, he had that feeling again. This was where he was meant to be. Close enough to be on hand if his sister and Sean needed him, far enough away from everyone else that he couldn't get drawn into village politics or other people's problems. And at a moment's notice, he could always jump off the deck down the steps at the back of the house and into the sea—or at least take out the little boat he kept tied up there.

It was perfect.

What *wasn't* perfect was whatever problem had brought Sean to his door.

He wanted a shower, and then he wanted peace and quiet to mull over what was going on with Rowan and her sister without having to worry that it would affect his life in any way. But what he *had* was a nephew who needed him, and coffee.

He sighed, and turned back to hand Sean his mug.

'Okay. What's going on?'

'It's Kayla,' Sean said.

'I could have guessed that.' Kayla was Sean's girlfriend of the last six months or so, and probably the only thing Uncle Gwyn might be more qualified to talk about than Sean's mum. Okay, not *qualified*. Comfortable, maybe.

He waited silently for his nephew to say more, but his mind was already working overtime. Was Kayla pregnant? Did Sean plan to propose? Was *she* pushing for him to propose? Had one of them cheated? Was she leaving the village for some reason? Or was there another argument he didn't know about, something causing tension between them?

'She thinks we should head to London and try and make it on the music scene there,' Sean said finally.

Gwyn's chest tightened. Of course she did. Of course she would.

He knew how serious Sean and Kayla were about their music. That was how they'd got together in the first place, performing together at the local pub's open mic night after weeks of watching each other up on stage. They were a great duo, and they both had real talent. Gwyn should be encouraging them.

But instead he said, 'You're not ready.'

Sean nodded dutifully. 'That's what I said. We need more songs first; we've got a few really great ones, but the rest are covers, and I want to go there with our strongest game.'

'Right,' Gwyn said, even though that wasn't what he'd meant at all.

'She figures we'll get inspired just by being there, though, being part of the scene,' Sean went on. 'Except we don't have the money for that. We'd be working all the time just to pay rent.'

'Exactly.' He hadn't meant that either. But Sean seemed to be talking himself out of the idea all on his own, which worked for him.

'So we shouldn't go yet, right?' Sean looked up at him with an uncertain gaze, the vulnerability in his face clear.

He trusted his uncle to tell him the truth. To offer advice in his best interests.

To put aside his own past to consider this situation.

It was only the last one Gwyn couldn't do.

He sighed. 'Look, I think you're right. London is tough, the music industry is tougher, and if you don't think you're ready for it, then you're not. Take the time and do it right.'

Or never. Never would work for Gwyn too.

He'd seen what the music industry could do to talented young men from Cornwall. He'd lived it. And his best friend hadn't survived it.

He and Darrell had been just like Sean and Kayla—well, musically, anyway. They'd been young and talented and determined to make it big, and they'd moved to London in search of fame and fortune. And they'd got lucky—after a lot of hard work. They'd got that coveted record deal eventually.

Yes, they'd been a success—there'd been albums and tours and billboards, for a time, anyway.

But there'd also been drugs and depression and death. And a life Gwyn could have had here in Rumbelow that had slipped through his fingers when he'd left, and he'd never been able to get back.

Was any of it worth it? Not in Gwyn's book. Fame brought misery, not just fortune. And he wouldn't wish it on anyone. Especially not one of the only two people in the world he still cared about.

Gwyn didn't like to mess with other people's lives. He didn't want to get involved. But in this case...

'You're doing the right thing, Sean,' he said. 'Stay here in Rumbelow.'

He had to keep his nephew safe. He couldn't let him walk the same path he had.

That was the only thing that mattered.

Telling Rowan the whole story took longer than Willow had expected—and required several cups of tea. But the basics—the unvarnished, unflattering, unimpressive basics—didn't change, no matter how she explained it.

She and Ben had met at that society party and realised they were a good fit—not personally, exactly, but in the eyes of all the people around them. They were the sort of partner the other needed by their side at functions and in paparazzi photos.

For her part, Ben was rich enough that she could be sure he wasn't just after her money, and he was successful enough that he wasn't intimidated by her fame—which had definitely been an issue in the past. They also had a lot of friends—or, well, acquaintances—in common, so it was inevitable they'd end up at a lot of the same events.

As far as she understood Ben's motives, the fact that she was universally acknowledged as being beautiful seemed to be enough for him.

So they went out on a date and got photographed by the paparazzi. So they went out on another one, and people started talking about them. And she liked that. She liked being seen with a popular, rich, intelligent man. It gave her a sort of cachet that just being beautiful had never achieved. As if people saw the way Ben looked at her and thought, *There must be something more to her.*

Except, she realised too late, all Ben *ever* saw was her looks.

She sighed and finished the story. 'And now it's two years later, and we've never really had a conversation about our future, or our feelings, or if we even like each other beyond spending time in the public eye together and having someone there to have sex with whenever we want to scratch that itch.'

'Do you want to?' Rowan asked, her brows knitted together as she tried to make sense of the mess Willow had made of her love life. 'I mean, do you want to tell him about the baby?

See if the two of you can be a real family together?'

Willow knew why she was asking the question. It was something neither of them had ever known. Their father had been out of the picture almost before they were born, and their mother hadn't exactly been mum of the year. She'd always been more interested in how much money they could make her than who they were inside.

Even Willow knew that. Rowan had been the one who couldn't take it, who'd run away because she needed more. Who'd never spoken to their mother since.

Willow... Willow had understood their mother better, she thought. And once she was a grown-up, and her mum had remarried and moved away, it seemed she'd found someone else to fulfil that role—of seeing Willow as a commodity, rather than a person.

God, how had it taken her so long to realise that?

'I...' Willow looked up and met Rowan's gaze, swallowing hard. 'It sounds awful, but I don't think I do. This is the man I spent the last two years of my life with, sort of. But I know—like, deep down, heart knowledge—that he'd be the wrong partner for me in this. That we wouldn't be happy—and neither would our kid.'

Just saying it out loud made it feel more real.

She might have screwed up in her relationship with Ben. She might have screwed up by getting pregnant in the first place.

But she didn't have to *keep* screwing up.

'You still need to tell him, though,' Rowan pointed out. 'Especially if… Wait. I skipped ahead a step. Do you know what you want to do? Do you want to keep the baby?'

That at least was an easy question.

The timing was terrible, the circumstances anything but ideal, the father not who she should have chosen…but she wanted this baby.

It was strange. Being a mother wasn't something she'd ever really spent much time thinking about, the same way she'd never really imagined her wedding the way some other girls seemed to. She'd assumed the wedding thing was because she got to wear incredible dresses every day in her job, so what was one more? The baby thing… It was just impossible to picture it in her life as she lived it.

But now it was here, growing inside her, none of that impossibility mattered. Because, one way or another, she was going to make it possible.

She was fortunate, she knew that. She had the money and the resources to make this far easier than most unplanned pregnancies turned out. But she also had an unexpected extra asset—a fierce, inexplicable love and fire that had shown up the moment the test turned positive that made her determined to do whatever it took to make sure this child had the best life she could give it.

'I do. And it might be crazy, because what about my career and my figure and my life, and I don't have any support in New York, but I guess I can hire that? I don't know. All I know is that I want to be a mum—a better one than ours was. I want to raise this baby right. And yes, I *know* I have to tell Ben. I just… I need to figure some things out first, about how this is all going to work.'

'I can get that.' Rowan smiled, as if she understood at last. But Willow knew she didn't really. Not yet.

She picked her words as carefully as she could. 'I just know if I talk to Ben before I've made some decisions about everything…he'll take over. He'll want things his way and I won't be sure enough of anything to fight him on it.'

Ben had what other men described as a 'forceful personality', the sort of trait that was useful in the boardroom, she supposed, but terrible in a supposedly equal relationship. He would make a split-second decision based on the information at hand, and that was it—it was done.

Usually, Willow was happy enough to go along with what he wanted, when it came to where to eat for dinner, or which party to go to, or where to holiday to best be seen together. But this...their child wasn't a PR stunt. And she was half afraid that if she told him, he'd have her halfway down the aisle before she'd finished the word *pregnant*.

She didn't want to marry Ben. That much she was one hundred per cent sure of.

Which meant she had to figure out what she *did* want, so she could give him that information straight, with no wiggle room for him to demand his own way. She'd discuss and debate with him, fine. But she wouldn't let herself be talked into something she didn't think was right.

So that was why she was here. To figure out what was right, before she talked to Ben.

Rowan reached across the table and grabbed her hand. 'You can stay here as long as you like,' she said, her voice fierce. 'We'll figure this all out so you can go back with a plan and do this the way you need to.'

Willow's face relaxed into a small smile. 'Thank you. That will really help.'

'Of course. You're my sister. I'll always be here for you.'

She hoped that was true. Because Willow wasn't done asking for what she needed yet. And even though she had a feeling that what she needed from her sister would end up being good for *both* of them, she was pretty sure Rowan wouldn't see it that way. At least, not to start with.

Rowan stood up and started towards the kettle again, but Willow stopped her with a gentle hand on her arm. 'Actually, there was one more thing I needed. It's a lot to ask, but…'

'Anything.'

'I need you to go to New York and pretend to be me. So Ben doesn't get suspicious. I need you to be Willow Harper, supermodel, for a few weeks.'

Gwyn was late going for his run the following day. And, actually, it was less of a run and more of a stroll into the village in a search for breakfast and coffee. Lots of coffee.

He'd slept badly after Sean's visit, memories of his own life in London, his own experiences of fame, swirling around in his head.

He'd tried to drown them out with a whisky or two, drunk straight from his best cut-glass crystal, sitting out on his balcony watching the ocean. Usually, the sea made him feel relaxed, the relentless motion of the waves reminding him that the world was constantly in flux and all things would pass.

Last night, it just made him feel queasy, so he'd called time and headed to bed, where his dreams had been haunted by Darrell, asking why he hadn't saved him, why he hadn't been there. Then he'd merged into his sister, Abigail, asking him the same thing. *'Where were you, Gwyn? I needed you.'*

And finally, perhaps not worst of all, but always last somehow, the gentle ghost of Rachel—not dead, but still gone—smiling sadly at him as she said, *'You weren't here. I had to deal with it and move on.'*

He'd given up on sleep early and tried to work for a couple of hours, before falling asleep at his desk and crawling back into bed to see if it would stick for a while.

When he'd finally dragged himself out again to shower, dress and head into the village, his day was already behind schedule. Not that he really needed to stick to one that much these days.

His time as a music star had made him richer than he'd ever imagined, and the money kept rolling in as his songs were played on radios and adverts and films and TV. He still worked, keeping his hand in the industry, but writing songs for other people instead of himself. Without Darrell at his side, he couldn't imagine performing again, but the music was still inside him and he needed to get it out somehow.

The early spring sunshine was weak but still warming as he walked along the cliff path towards the town. His house, sitting just past the harbour, had a path down across the beach in low tide, or around the boats in high, but he usually preferred to climb the steps at the back of the house up to the clifftop and walk down that way. Less chance of bumping into people, except Rowan.

The locals at Rumbelow had welcomed him home without a fuss when he'd returned from London. They'd all known him since birth, remembered his parents before they passed, knew his sister well, and had stories of the scrapes he'd got into as a child. But they'd known Darrell the same way, and they all felt his loss too. So nobody had pushed, nobody had asked questions, and if they talked about

what had happened, they did it behind his back,
which at least meant he didn't have to hear it.

They'd just accepted him back and never
blamed him—but they'd never really trusted
him again either. Gwyn knew he wasn't one
of them any more.

Another reason to stay out at his cliff house.

Once he'd found breakfast and coffee.

The village was busy at mid-morning, full
of shoppers picking up pastries and freshly
baked bread, people meeting for coffee, early
tourists making the most of the sunshine before the promised rain later. The fishermen, of
course, had been out at sea for hours already,
but soon they'd be returning with the fresh
catch, ready for the local pubs and restaurants
to cook it for lunch.

In the winter the village hibernated, shrink-
ing down to just the locals—or at least the
people who lived there all year round. The
holiday homes stood empty, the local caravan
parks and camping sites closed for the season, and the weather drew in, dissuading day-
trippers from visiting too.

Winter was the time to stay in, stay warm,
and wait it out. But now, in the spring, the village was coming to life again. By the middle of
summer he wouldn't be able to get a table at his

favourite café for all the tourists queuing out of the door, but right now there was a seat at the window counter just waiting for him, and the waitress, Michelle, nodded to him as he took it. In no time at all, he had both a coffee and the bacon sandwich he'd been craving. The sandwich went down fast, but he took some time savouring the coffee. It was even better than the stuff from his high-end machine back at the house.

As he sat there, looking out over the village square, he spotted someone who looked both familiar and out of place at the same time, and smiled. Rowan.

Or maybe not.

Usually, his neighbour favoured bright and colourful clothes, or at least relaxed and comfortable ones. Today, she appeared to be wearing designer jeans, heeled boots, a white sweater and a tan leather jacket—the same one he'd seen tossed over a suitcase the day before. The clothes themselves didn't look overly ostentatious, but somehow the sleek and groomed outfit still gave the impression of money. As did her perfectly styled hair, make-up and designer sunglasses.

The fact she looked completely lost was a bit of a giveaway too.

He ducked his head as she turned towards the café so she didn't see him, then smiled as he watched her feet move towards the door and heard the bell tinkle. Glancing up from behind his menu, he saw her scan the room then head straight for the counter.

'Rowan, take a seat, honey, and I'll bring your tea right over,' Michelle called to her. 'You want a *pain au chocolat* with that?'

Not-Rowan's eyes widened. 'Oh, I was just going to get a takeaway coffee...' she started, but Michelle had moved on and wasn't listening—which meant she didn't hear the transatlantic twang to her voice either.

Yep. Definitely not Rowan. But she hadn't corrected Michelle either, which meant she probably wanted people to think she was.

She stood uncertainly by the counter for another moment, which made Gwyn smile. She didn't look like the sort of woman who was *ever* usually uncertain.

In fact, if he was correct, this woman was used to people scampering around, catering to her every whim. Because if he was right—and by now he was pretty certain he was—this woman was Rowan's sister, supermodel Willow Harper.

Which begged the question, what the hell

was she doing in Rumbelow? And why was she pretending to be Rowan?

There was only one way to find out, really.

He turned to Willow and raised a hand, beckoning her over. He figured, if she was trying to pretend to be her sister, she'd have to acknowledge her neighbour.

The indecision was clear on her face, and Gwyn hid a smile at the sight. Really, what *was* she playing at? As much as he tried to stay out of other people's issues, he had to admit he was intrigued.

Finally, she came and took the stool beside him at the window. 'Hi…uh… Gwyn.'

'Hello, *Rowan*.' If she noticed the extra emphasis he put on the name, she didn't mention it. She was still looking hopefully towards the waitress.

If he was right, she was going to be disappointed.

'It's a lovely morning out there, isn't it?' he said, jerking his head towards the window. 'Spring has definitely arrived.'

When in doubt, talk about the weather. It was the British way, after all.

'Yes. Lovely.' She gave him a tight smile.

'How's that herb garden coming on?' Gwyn had no real interest in gardening, but he knew

Rowan had been sweating over trying to keep herbs alive recently because she'd complained to him about it often enough.

'Fantastic,' she responded. 'Growing like, um, weeds.'

That seemed unlikely. More proof this wasn't really Rowan.

Awkward silence stretched between them until Michelle bustled over with Rowan's usual tea tray. She plonked it down on the counter in front of her and Gwyn watched her pull a face at it.

'More of a coffee girl these days, huh?' he said.

'Oh, no, you know me. I love my tea,' she said, entirely unconvincingly.

'Of course you do.' Gwyn swallowed the last of his own coffee, then pulled out his wallet. Leaving enough to cover both orders, he got to his feet and smiled down at her.

'Come on, *Rowan*. If you're after coffee, I've got a great machine at my place.' He lowered his voice. 'And maybe once we're in private you can explain to me exactly why you're here in Rumbelow pretending to be my neighbour.'

CHAPTER THREE

FOR A SPLIT second Willow considered continu-
ing the charade, but it was clear Gwyn wasn't
going to buy it. When she'd asked Rowan about
her neighbour the night before, she'd said he
was nice enough but they weren't really close.
But apparently he thought there was more to
their friendship than she did—that or he was
just incurably nosy. Either way, he was a problem. One she had to solve if she didn't want this
whole scheme to be over before it even started.

So she nodded and stood up, letting him
hold the door open for her as she stepped out
into the spring sunlight.

If he wasn't going to buy their story, then
she needed a better one. And she figured she
had the length of the walk back to the lifeboat
station to come up with one.

She really wished she'd had her one morning coffee already. It could only have helped.

The walk up the hill out of the village wasn't

a long one, but it took long enough for Willow to mentally run through all her options.

Option One: call the whole thing off. Rowan would be at the airport by now, but her flight wouldn't have left. She could call her, tell her the jig was up and get her to head home. Give her back her passport and go back to hiding out in her cottage.

Except Willow didn't want to call her back. Convincing her to go in the first place had been hard enough. If she showed any sign of weakness Rowan would be back in a flash. And, as much as she was doing this for her own reasons, a little part of it was for Rowan too. Her twin had spent too many years isolated and alone here. It was time for her to get back out into the world again.

And Willow needed that same space and isolation to think, here in Rumbelow, away from Ben. Which meant Ben couldn't have any reason to think she wasn't in New York. Even though they were technically split up right now, she knew he'd be keeping tabs on her—and she was an easy person to keep tabs on, usually. She didn't have any shows or shoots planned for the next few weeks—much to Rowan's relief. But in a normal week she'd definitely get papped by a passing photographer and end up with her picture in the gossip mags or on the internet. All Rowan would have to do was take a walk through Central Park once a week, or maybe go shopping, and they'd be covered. Ben would believe she was still in New York, and he'd leave her be.

He'd be waiting for her to call and beg him to come back. Not that she'd ever done that before, but in his head she was sure that was what her texting to ask if he was free for a party or a premiere would amount to. Or her saying yes when he did the same. Either way, he'd be expecting her to be at his beck and call.

Rowan would probably do a better job of saying no to him than she ever had, anyway.

She didn't know how he got under her skin the way he did, but it was a talent he'd honed over their years together. With everyone else she felt confident, together and capable of anything. But with Ben...

But she didn't have to deal with Ben right now. Right now, she needed to handle Gwyn. And he *had* to be easier to manage than Ben, right?

The salt air floating in from the sea helped to clear her mind, and she moved onto Option Two.

Tell Gwyn the truth. Come clean about who

she was and hope that he'd help her. After all, Rowan said he was a good guy, and he'd obviously already figured most of it out. Maybe he'd be willing to help her keep her cover for the rest of the village.

Apparently she was going to need some help if she wanted to pass as her sister. Being literally identical didn't seem to be enough.

If nothing else, she was going to have to learn to love tea again.

There was an Option Three, she supposed—stay here in Rumbelow as Willow, not Rowan, and hope nobody said anything. But it felt like a bit too much to ask for an entire village to keep a secret. Besides, it was spring, and tourists were starting to arrive, from what she'd seen that morning. Someone would be sure to say something.

The two things she had In her favour were the fact that nobody expected to see a world-famous supermodel in a tiny Cornish village, and the fact that nobody really looked the same off camera as they did on. Without the photo retouching, the filters, the make-up and hair-styling, not to mention the incredible outfits, even Willow barely looked like Willow Harper.

She just needed to do a better job of looking like Rowan.

As they turned the next bend in the path and the village fell away, Rowan's cottage came into view. Gwyn paused for a second as they approached.

'Do we need to stop and get her too?'

Willow didn't bother pretending she didn't know who he meant. It was already clear the jig was up and Option Four—tell him he was wrong and try to style the whole thing out—wasn't going to work.

She shook her head. 'She's already gone.'

Gwyn nodded and kept walking. 'You know I'm going to be asking where, very soon.' His voice was tight, and she realised he was genuinely concerned for her sister, and whatever scheme Willow had got her caught up in.

Which, now she thought about it, was fair enough.

'When we get inside,' she replied. She didn't think it was likely anyone was hanging out on the cliffs listening in, but she wasn't going to chance it. Besides, she still needed to find the right words to explain everything, without making herself sound like she'd lost her grip on reality.

Explaining the plan to Rowan had been one thing. She'd been concerned, maybe confused, but Willow had always known her sister would come through for her in the end.

Trying to explain it to someone else…she wasn't sure quite how sane it would sound.

The cliff path turned again, one last bend leading them to a steep staircase attached to the rock. Gwyn hopped down them nimbly, with the obvious practice of having done this every day for who knew how long. Willow took them rather more gingerly. The last thing she needed now was to fall and break her leg.

Or worse. Hurt the baby.

She swallowed, and focused harder on where she placed her feet.

She wasn't used to it yet, the feeling of being more than just herself. Of having to worry about someone who couldn't take care of themselves. Who was so entirely reliant on her own body to even exist.

And that feeling was here to stay, she knew. Right now, all she had to do was eat right, rest, take the vitamins the internet said she needed, and not fall over. In just over six months' time, she was going to need to do a heck of a lot more.

Gwyn swept ahead to open what she realised must be the back door to the place, which led them into a wide, wooden-floored open-plan kitchen, dining and living space.

Willow wasn't looking at theIr, though. She was captivated by the view.

Huge frameless windows opened out straight onto the ocean, the glass almost disappearing until it felt as if she hovered over the waves. Without realising she was doing it, Willow moved straight to the edge, one hand resting against the glass as the sun shimmered on the water below.

There was no sign of any doors off the downstairs space, but a compact spiral staircase led up to a mezzanine floor above, where she assumed the sleeping and bathing areas must be. The upper floor came not quite to the window, but close enough to make the most of the view.

Imagine waking up to this every morning.

Her own Manhattan penthouse had its own charms, and a view out over the city and Central Park was certainly one of them. But this... this was magical.

How had she stayed away from England for so long?

'I can see why Rowan came here,' she murmured.

Behind her, coffee cups clinked and she heard the welcome sound of a coffee machine whirring, pouring hot, dark caffeine into the china. Moments later, Gwyn appeared at her side, holding out a cup towards her.

'Does that mean you're ready to tell me who you really are, and why you're pretending to be my neighbour?' He held the cup just out of reach until she nodded.

'But we'd better sit down,' she said, taking the coffee. 'It's a bit of a story.'

Gwyn tried to keep his expression blank as he listened to her story. Some of it he'd already figured out for himself—that she was Willow, Rowan's twin, and that she needed to lie low for a while so was hiding out in Rumbelow.

Other parts of the story took him rather more by surprise.

'Wait. You convinced *Rowan* to go to New York and pretend to be *you*?' He hoped to God she was doing a better job of it than Willow was here in Rumbelow. But still, the idea of his reclusive, homebody neighbour jetting off to New York to live the high life was sort of unbelievable. Rowan didn't even like having to go into the next *town* to go shopping. She ordered everything she could on the internet— he knew because he ended up with her parcels when she wasn't home. But even then he knew she was never further away than the village or the beach.

Rowan didn't go places.

Until now, apparently.

Willow pulled a face. 'It took some doing. But… I think it'll be good for her. She was stagnating here in Cornwall.'

'Stagnating,' Gwyn repeated. 'Is that what you think?'

She seemed to realise too late that she might have offended him. 'Oh, I mean, it's a gorgeous place, and I can absolutely see why anyone would want to live here. Well, not me. But Rowan, for sure. It's just, when she came here…she was running away. This was her hiding place. And it's just that it's been six years. She has to come out of hiding eventually, doesn't she?'

'I don't know,' Gwyn admitted. 'I don't know what she was hiding from.' Some things you had to hide from for ever, he supposed.

Willow tipped her head to the side. 'I thought you two were friends.'

'We are,' he said with a shrug. 'I guess. Just not the "confess our darkest secrets over bottles of wine" friends. More, "Can you take the bins out for me while I'm away?" friends. Except she's never away, so that one's just me.'

Maybe they weren't friends. Maybe they were just convenient acquaintances.

'Hmm.' She seemed to be re-evaluating how much she could trust him. 'But you knew I wasn't Rowan, so you must know her pretty well. No one else noticed.'

He couldn't help but scoff at that. 'They would have done. Rowan always thought no one knew who she was either, but they did. They just didn't want to bring it up and embarrass her.' Not when she was so clearly trying to go incognito. And after a while she was just part of the village, anyway.

'Oh.' Willow's eyes were wide as she digested that information. 'So, what gave me away?'

'You mean, apart from ordering coffee instead of tea? I don't know… Your clothes, your accent, your everything. Plus, don't forget, I saw both of you at the same time yesterday. That was a pretty big giveaway.'

She winced. 'Yeah. So…are you going to tell everyone who I am?'

'Why would I?' Gwyn sat back in his chair and folded his arms over his chest as he studied her. She was tense, sitting right on the edge of her seat, her back perfectly straight. Maybe that was just model posture, but maybe not.

If he had to bet on it, he'd say she was scared—of something or someone. But what? Or who?

'I don't like to get involved in other people's business,' he said slowly, and she huffed a laugh before looking away. 'Yeah, okay, I can see how it might not seem like that. But usually, I stay as far away from other people's issues as I can—ask anyone. Maybe *that's* why Rowan and I aren't "sharing" friends.'

'Then why are you so worked up about me being here, pretending to be her for a few weeks?'

It was a fair question, and one Gwyn wasn't entirely sure he had a good answer to.

'I just hate to see anybody doing something so badly,' he said, mostly to buy himself time.

She snorted. 'Fine. You want to coach me on how to be my sister?'

'No. I want you to tell me why you're even trying.' The words came out without thought, without intention for sure. He didn't care what her problems were, and he sure as hell didn't want to get involved.

Except…he'd saved her from embarrassed explanations in the café, and he'd brought her home for coffee. So maybe he cared a little bit, despite himself.

Somehow, he suspected this was his nephew's fault, or maybe his sister's. They kept trying to get him more involved in things, to the point of even asking him for *advice*. Yeah, this was probably their fault.

Willow's eyes had narrowed and she was studying him carefully, obviously deciding what to tell him. Which meant whatever she was planning wasn't the truth. Well, he didn't have the time or energy for lies.

'Don't bother trying to sell me on some "it's all for her own good" scheme,' he said casually. 'We both know you wouldn't be here if you weren't running or hiding from something. So, if you want me to help you, tell me what it is. If you don't…' he shrugged '…finish your coffee and we'll talk about the weather. It's no skin off my nose. Just don't bother lying to me. Okay?'

Willow gave a slow nod, sighed, then put her coffee cup down on the small table between them.

'It goes without saying that this has to stay just between the two of us, right?' She sounded suddenly far more serious, and more weary, than she had before.

Gwyn nodded. 'Trust me, I don't tell my own family what's going on with me. I'm not about to start gossiping about you.'

'Good. Because…you're right. I *am* hiding out here. And I asked Rowan to go to New York and be seen there so that people—one person, really—would think I was still in the city. Because I need to take some time away to think and decide what to do next. Because, you see…' she swallowed so hard he saw her throat move '… I'm pregnant.'

Gwyn looked so astonished she felt obliged to add, 'It's not yours, don't worry,' in her driest voice.

He chuckled at that, which made her feel a little better.

Here she was, outing her biggest secret to a virtual stranger, and he just looked horrified. Why? Did he think she was going to be a terrible mother? Well, yes, he probably *did* think that since the only thing he knew about her was that she'd conned her own sister into leaving the safety of this village to fly to New York and assume a fake identity, and she was drinking strong coffee while pregnant and hiding from the father of her child.

She dropped the cup into the saucer. At least the caffeine thing she could do something about. The websites said *some* coffee was fine, and she'd been trying to stick to that, but right now she couldn't remember how much counted as some and this stuff was really strong, and really she needed to *know* these things. Mothers knew things, didn't they?

She wished she hadn't sent Rowan away. She really didn't want to be alone in this.

But she had. So all she had now was... Gwyn. Who was still looking at her as if she might be playing a practical joke on him.

Then his expression hardened. 'So you've come here to—what? Get rid of it without the father knowing? Pretend it's Rowan's baby and give it up for adoption? What?'

'No!' Okay, she might not have made the best first impression here, but that was quite a leap in logic, wasn't it? Willow suspected he had his own reasons for jumping to such conclusions, but for now she just needed to focus on setting the story straight. The last thing she needed was him going to the papers with his assumptions. 'Oh, God.' She slumped down in her chair. 'That's exactly what the gossip sites are going to assume if they find out I'm here, pretending to be my sister, aren't they?' Those sites always assumed the worst, especially about her.

The more famous you were, the further you

had to fall. And they just loved pulling people down.

'I'd imagine so,' Gwyn said, still watching her carefully, presumably waiting for a real explanation. 'You know how those sites are.'

And so did he, she realised from the bitterness in his voice. How? When had he been on the wrong side of their sharp tongues?

A question for another time. But definitely another layer to explore.

She was just as guilty of making assumptions about him as he was about her. She'd assumed Rowan's neighbour would be a local boy— made good, somehow, to afford this house, but still part of the community, never wanting to be anywhere else, everybody's best friend.

But the more she got to know him, the more she wondered if there was another story here she was missing. One she maybe should already know.

Right now, though, she had to challenge his assumptions about *her*.

'I came here because I needed time and space to think,' she explained. 'Not about the baby, exactly—I know I want to keep it and I'm in the fortunate position where I can afford to look after us both whatever happens next. But about the baby's father.'

'You don't want to tell him?' Gwyn guessed.

'I know I need to,' she said. 'And I wouldn't keep that information from someone, not long-term. I just… I don't think we should raise the child together.'

Now Gwyn's posture changed—from the defensive arms across the chest pose he'd been in since she'd first mentioned the pregnancy, to leaning forward, his wrists resting on his knees. 'Is this… Are you scared of him?'

It wasn't quite the same question Rowan had asked, and for some reason it gave her pause. *Was* she scared of Ben?

Yes. Yes, she was.

Just not in the way Gwyn probably meant.

'I don't think he'll hurt me, if that's what you mean,' she said slowly. 'Or the baby. That's not the sort of man he is.'

'Then what sort of man is he?' Gwyn didn't seem to have relaxed any at her words. As if he knew as well as she did that violence wasn't all of it.

'He's used to getting his own way. And he… he expects to make all the decisions.'

'You're worried he's going to offer to "do the right thing by you",' Gwyn said. 'And you don't want to.'

The right thing. What even *was* that anyway? Oh, she knew what Gwyn meant—and what Ben probably would too. That they'd get married and give the kid two stable parents and she'd probably have to give up work and push swings or bake cookies or something.

The right thing, in Ben's eyes, would be a child born legitimately inside wedlock who could inherit the family business after him, and who he could pressurise and torment and belittle the same way his father had him.

And there was no way in hell that Willow was letting that happen.

She sighed and rubbed a hand across her forehead. 'It's complicated. His family...they have a lot of expectations. And yes, he probably would expect that we'd get married. And no, one thing this whole situation has made abundantly clear to me is that I don't want to marry him.'

She could hear Ben's voice in her head now, telling her that most women would be begging him for a ring, under the circumstances. She knew some of his past girlfriends had even tried to get pregnant to trap him into marriage—at least, according to him.

But she wasn't most women.

'So, what *do* you want?' Gwyn asked.

Willow looked up and met his steady gaze

with her own troubled one. 'I guess that's what I'm here in Rumbelow to figure out.'

Gwyn held her gaze for a long moment before sitting back and nodding to himself.

He was sure she wasn't telling him everything—hardly anybody ever did, and it wasn't as if they were best friends. He barely knew this woman. But as much as his usual instincts were telling him to run—to send her on her way with good wishes and then stay the hell out of her way for the rest of her visit to Rumbelow—there was another part of him that wanted something else.

It wanted to *fix* things for her.

He tried to fight down that part, silently reminding himself of every other time he'd tried to fix things for someone, and how every single time things had fallen apart until they were worse than before.

It wasn't just trying to save Darrell from himself in London. Or not being there in Rumbelow to save Abigail when she'd needed him, even if he knew she'd never have let him. It wasn't even everything that had happened in between with Rachel, not really—even if the baby talk had instantly brought her to mind.

It was all of those things put together, he

supposed. All of them telling him that he was safer—that *everyone* was better off—if he let people live their own lives. Make their own mistakes.

Because even when he tried to intervene, to help, he only made things worse. And if he didn't let himself get involved, he wouldn't hate himself when it all inevitably went to hell.

He could already see exactly how this whole thing with Willow was going to play out, like a movie trailer in his head that gave away the whole plot in sixty seconds.

He'd go against his better instincts, give in to those big blue eyes and that lost and lonely smile, and help Willow—especially since she was all alone here in the village, vulnerable, and very likely to give herself away in about thirty seconds if he didn't. He'd challenge *anyone* not to help her.

So he'd show her around, get to know her, probably ferry her to doctors' appointments, that sort of thing. He'd listen to her worries, try to offer helpful advice or at least show her she had more options than she thought. He'd probably introduce her to Abigail, since his sister was definitely better at that sort of thing than he was.

And he'd grow to like her, he was sure. She

seemed a likeable person, against the odds. He'd assumed famous supermodels would be, well, less approachable at least. Living in a different sphere of reality, perhaps. But she just seemed like a normal person, grappling with the problems of life.

He wouldn't fall in love with her—at least he didn't have to worry about that. Love wasn't really a word in his vocabulary any more—not romantic love, anyway. If he was sensible, he wouldn't let himself grow too close at all, knowing she wouldn't be staying—she'd be gone before the summer, he would bet.

Still, life would tick along and he'd help her out and feel as if he was a useful, valuable human being again for a change.

And then it would all fall apart—because it always did.

Maybe she'd go back to the boyfriend, get married, even though she knew it was the wrong thing for her.

Maybe she'd decide she wasn't cut out to be a mother and give the baby up for adoption—or farm it out to a nanny so she didn't have to be involved.

Maybe she'd realise her real life was waiting somewhere else and leave without a backward glance or a second thought.

Or maybe there was something even worse waiting around the corner for her, or for him. Heaven only knew how many times the universe had blindsided him with worse things than even his nightmares gave him.

Something would happen, and he'd be left picking up the pieces. And someone would say to him, not for the first or second or even third time in his life, *You shouldn't have got involved.*

He *tried* not to get involved. He knew how it ended.

But he looked up at Willow again, watched her worrying at her bottom lip with her teeth, twirling her blonde ponytail around one hand, and he knew that wasn't going to matter.

He sighed. 'I don't suppose you've got a doctor sorted out over here yet, have you? I've got a mate over in the next town who's a midwife. Might be more discreet than going to Dr Fenton here in Rumbelow.' Especially since Dr Fenton was a hundred years old and a notorious gossip, despite all his protestations of patient confidentiality. 'I can make a call.'

Willow smiled. 'That would be wonderful. Thank you.'

CHAPTER FOUR

IT WAS POSSIBLE that Willow hadn't thought this plan all the way through before she'd put her sister on a plane to New York.

For instance, being pregnant meant things like doctors' visits and hospital scans and not eating some things and eating others, and basically it felt like it might actually be a full-time job, just growing another human. Which she supposed made sense, when she thought of it that way.

Gwyn laughed when she mentioned it to him the following week as they drove out of the village together—the long way round, to avoid any gossip if they were seen driving through the village square together, heading off on an adventure.

'You'd be amazed what people will gossip about around here,' he'd told her as his car took the path away from Rumbelow.

'I thought Rowan said one of things she liked

most about this place was that people *didn't* talk about her,' Willow had replied, confused.

'Not to her face, no,' Gwyn had said.

'Ah.' After that, she'd watched the sea fall away behind the cliffs as they turned inland towards the next town, and Gwyn's midwife friend.

It was fortunate that she'd never given up her British citizenship—it had made registering for medical care in the UK far easier than she'd expected. She'd considered just using Rowan's doctor and assuming her identity for this too, but that felt like a step too far, even for her.

She'd planned—as much as she'd planned anything—to go private. But private care this deep into Cornwall appeared to be more remote than she'd imagined, and even the nearest hospital was a serious drive away. And Gwyn's midwife friend had, against the odds, been able to fit her in without too much of a wait. So, in the end, this had just been easier.

Except, of course, she didn't have a car. It would have been kind of conspicuous to call for one of her drivers to pick her up, and according to Gwyn the local taxi driver—singular—gossiped worse than the doctor, so in the end she'd had to accept his offer to take her.

'I guess it's not the kind of job you're used to,' Gwyn said, referring to her earlier comment. 'Growing a baby, I mean.'

'Not exactly,' Willow replied drily. 'My job usually involves staying slim and—if possible—slimmer. Not growing at all.'

He glanced over at her then, his eyes only leaving the road for a second, but long enough for her to see something unexpected flash in them.

'You know, a lot of men find a pregnant woman very sexy.'

'And you're one of them, I suppose?' At least it would explain why he was being so helpful. Otherwise, she was building up a debt she was rather afraid her sister was going to have to pay when she got back.

But Gwyn shrugged. 'I've never really been around enough of them to find out. Except my sister, and she *really* doesn't count.'

'No, I can't imagine she would.' Willow pulled a face. 'But my job isn't to be sexy anyway, not really. It's to make the clothes look good.'

'You make yourself sound like a glorified coat hanger,' Gwyn pointed out.

She shrugged. 'Maybe. The point is, the clothes aren't made to fit a pregnant body. So

I'm not going to be working for a little while. Which means I might as well concentrate on doing *this*.' She waved a hand around the centre of her body.

She knew she sounded nonchalant, even dismissive, about the whole thing. But that was how she dealt with it. Inside, maybe somewhere around where her baby sat, she was fizzing—with excitement and fear and anticipation and apprehension. She *wanted* this baby, more than she'd thought was possible before she'd found out she was having it.

But she also had no idea how to be a mother—especially a single mother—without screwing up. Her own hadn't exactly been a shining example.

The rest of the winding drive through the Cornish countryside passed in silence. Willow stared out of the window, ostensibly enjoying the views, but by the time Gwyn pulled into the car park at the doctor's surgery she couldn't have told him any of the things she'd seen. Her mind was elsewhere, on tiny fingers clutching hers, with no one else in the world to depend on.

'You okay about this?' Gwyn asked, and she realised suddenly that the engine was off and he was waiting for her to unfasten her seatbelt.

She took a breath. 'I think I have to be, don't I?'

That was the thing about babies. Doubts didn't stop them coming.

Not doubts. I want this. Just... Worry. Fear.

But Willow Harper had never let being afraid stop her before. So she pressed the button to release her seatbelt and opened the car door just before Gwyn darted around to do it for her.

Inside, the waiting room was busy. Willow hung back behind Gwyn as he headed to the desk to tell the receptionist they'd arrived. She really didn't want to be noticed or recognised here and she'd dressed accordingly—in a faded pair of jeans with a striped T-shirt and an oversized cardigan of her sister's, along with baseball shoes. With her hair up, her shoulders hunched and her face dipped, the odds were she'd look just like a thousand women. At least that was the hope. Gwyn hadn't looked convinced when she'd explained about her disguise.

Now, Willow scanned the room from under the brim of the baseball cap she'd found in the depths of Rowan's wardrobe, but luckily everyone seemed preoccupied enough with whatever reason *they* had for being there that day to pay too much attention to the new couple who'd just arrived.

Couple. Oh.

Everyone here was going to think they were a couple, weren't they? If they realised she was here to see the midwife, they'd assume Gwyn was the father. Even his friend would probably think the same, unless he'd explained. Even if he *had* explained they might suspect. She wondered if that had occurred to him yet.

There were forms to fill in, of course—lots of them. Willow hesitated only for a moment before putting her real name down rather than her twin's. Gwyn noticed, though, she was sure. She could tell by the way he watched her hawkishly until she wrote, then turned away, looking satisfied, and stretched his legs out in front of him.

'It shouldn't be too long,' he said, although Willow had no idea how he could possibly know that.

In the end, he was right, though. Her name was called just a few minutes later.

'Do you want me to come in with you?' he asked.

She did, she realised. She didn't want to be doing this alone.

But coping alone was something she was going to have to get used to, if she didn't want Ben to be a regular part of her life any more.

Maybe that was what she was really doing here in Cornwall. Testing the water to see if she could make it on her own.

Which meant not leaning on her sister's friendly neighbour any more than was strictly necessary. However appealing that idea might be.

'No,' she said finally, after too long of a pause to be convincing. 'You stay here. Otherwise, no one will ever believe you're not the father.'

He huffed a laugh at that. 'Fair point.' He sat back with his arms folded as she turned away, paperwork in hand, and walked towards the midwife's room.

But she felt his gaze on her the whole way.

Gwyn didn't really know what to expect from Willow's visit to the midwife—and he got the impression that she didn't either. She'd been nervous and distracted in the car, then fidgeting with the pen in the waiting room as she'd filled in the forms, but she'd told him not to go in with her so he hadn't.

'Otherwise, no one will ever believe you're not the father.'

It hadn't occurred to him that people would jump to that conclusion, not least because she'd only been in the country a few days and he hadn't met her before. But if people thought she was Rowan, they wouldn't know that. They'd think they were friends—maybe friends with benefits.

Of course that was the conclusion people were going to jump to—especially back in Rumbelow—once the news of the pregnancy got out.

Another reason he shouldn't have got involved.

He settled back into his uncomfortable plastic waiting room chair and waited.

Too late now.

In the end, she was much quicker than he'd expected.

'It was mostly just about getting set up and registered,' Willow explained as she hurried past him out of the building. 'She's given me some information, and taken some details from me, that sort of thing. I'm to make another appointment according to the schedule in the file, and get booked in for a scan at the hospital.' She waved a green folder vaguely.

'Don't you want to do that now?' Gwyn asked as the door swung shut behind them. 'I mean, the reception desk is right in there, and getting through on the phone can be a nightmare...'

But Willow shook her head firmly, already striding towards the car.

Gwyn hesitated for a moment, then followed. But he didn't unlock the car, not quite yet.

She looked rattled, that was the only word for it. And if they got back in the car and he started driving they'd never talk about it—or she'd have some sort of massive breakdown in the middle of the road and he'd have to pull over and deal with it there.

Playing the odds, he'd rather deal with it now.

'What happened?' he asked as he approached where she stood, leaning against the passenger side door.

'I told you. Just forms and information and setting things up. There's not much they really need to do at this point, apart from schedule my probably very overdue twelve-week scan—the dates are a little...uncertain. Anyway. It's just...it's just all up to me.'

Her voice cracked on the last few words, and understanding rushed in.

'You're feeling overwhelmed.'

She arched an eyebrow at him. 'You don't think I *should* be? I'm entirely responsible for growing another human here, Gwyn.'

'And you just realised that if you don't go back to your boyfriend soon and come clean, you're going to be doing that all alone,' he guessed. Yeah, he could see how that would send a person spiralling.

He barely liked being responsible for himself, these days. Being responsible for other people... Just the idea made him shudder, given how badly he'd failed at it in the past.

Which was why he couldn't offer to make this any easier for Willow. If she was doing this, she was doing it alone—he certainly wasn't going to promise to be there for her, not on a few days' acquaintance and a passing friendship with her sister. It wasn't his baby, she wasn't his girlfriend—he was just a neighbour with a car and a friend who happened to be a midwife. That was all.

And he wasn't going to let it be any more, no matter how his gut told him to step in, to help, to comfort her.

He knew what lay that way, and he wasn't starting on that path.

'It's just...' Willow took a long, shuddering

breath. 'It's just a lot. And my scan probably won't be for another couple of weeks, so until then all I've got is the internet for support.'

'There are probably…' he waved his hand around vaguely '…books, or something? You could order?'

'Yeah. Books.' She gave him a wobbly smile. 'That's a good idea.'

But he knew it wasn't enough. This woman needed more than a bookshop. She needed support. And she'd sent away the one person who'd be best at giving that to her.

Which meant she needed a replacement. She needed a friend.

'Thank you for bringing me today,' she said. 'I know it was an inconvenience. I'll sort something else out for the scan appointment, don't worry.'

Gwyn's jaw tightened with the effort of not promising to take her.

I'm not getting involved, remember? At least, not more involved.

'But I'm really glad I didn't have to do today alone.' This time, her smile was a little stronger—which was why it took him so much by surprise when she lurched forward and hugged him.

He hadn't expected her to fit so well into his

arms. He was a tall man, and he wasn't used to women being the same height as him—at least, not when he was holding them. But her chin sat neatly on his shoulder, the fresh floral scent of her hair filling his lungs as he rested his cheek against it. She didn't cling on, didn't use him for support, just held him close—and Gwyn felt something dangerous twinging inside his chest.

Not getting involved, he reminded himself.

Willow pulled back and smiled at him again. 'Thanks.' She tucked a loose bit of hair behind her ear and glanced down at the ground. 'I'm not usually much of a hugger but, well, I needed that. Hormones, I guess.'

'Hormones. Right.' That made sense. It wasn't about him, she just needed a warm body to hug.

Which didn't change how stupidly glad he was that he'd been the warm body in closest proximity.

Gwyn gave himself a mental pep talk as they got into the car and he pulled out of the car park, back onto the country roads that would lead them home. He'd done a good deed for his temporary neighbour, bringing her here. He'd got a hug of thanks, and now he was done. That was all.

Okay, maybe he'd use his Amazon Prime account to send her a copy of whatever that pregnancy book was that always showed up in movies, because he suspected she wouldn't bother, and maybe it would help.

But that was definitely it. No more getting involved after that.

The familiar twists and turns of the roads grounded him, although he took them a little slower than usual with Willow in the car beside him. She seemed lost in thought too, staring back out of the window again. He wondered briefly what she was thinking about—then pushed the thought aside. Her thoughts were none of his business.

Probably the baby, though. Or what she was going to do next. The father sounded like a piece of work, from the little she'd told him. Any guy who would make a woman want to travel thousands of miles just to be sure she could figure out her own wants and needs without him trying to pressure her couldn't exactly be perfect marriage material.

Not that he could really talk, after Rachel.

And he was getting involved again.

Despite his slower speed, they made good time and before long he was pulling up in front of Rowan's little cottage to let her out.

'I suppose I'd better go figure out what there is left to eat in here,' Willow said as she climbed out of the car. 'I think I might have finished off all of Rowan's supplies, but I've got a grocery order coming tomorrow, I hope.'

One thing the tourist trade had brought to their remote area—regular supermarket deliveries. Something to be thankful for, Gwyn supposed.

But it wouldn't solve her food problem tonight. Her appointment had been late afternoon, and by now most of the shops in town would be shut. She could probably get takeaway, or put something together from whatever was in the back of Rowan's cupboards. Or...

Gwyn sighed.

He wasn't getting involved. He *wasn't*.

But he wasn't about to watch a pregnant woman starve either.

'I was going to grab dinner at the Star and Dragon in town,' he said. 'It's folk night—usually a good night. You're welcome to join me if you like.'

She gave him a wary look. 'As Rowan? Is that... Does she normally go there?'

Gwyn shrugged. 'I've never seen her there. She, uh, mostly keeps to herself, I think. I don't think anyone in the village really knows her that well.'

'But the woman in the café…she knew her regular order. She brought it over, even when I tried to order something else.'

'Yeah, well, that's just good business,' Gwyn explained. 'I mean, yes, people know her in the café and in the local shops, but only…superficially.' The same way he knew her, he supposed.

'Sometimes it feels like that's the only way anyone knows anyone else in New York,' Willow said with a sad smile. 'So you don't think anyone would notice I wasn't Rowan, if I went?'

He looked her over. Even dressed down to be incognito, she'd stand out anywhere. 'We'll stay in the corner,' he promised. 'So, you coming?'

She took a breath as if she were steeling herself, and he could actually see her resolve hardening. 'Just give me twenty minutes to get ready.'

It was closer to half an hour before Willow was ready to go, but since it took Gwyn even longer to get home, showered, changed—and pick up what looked like a guitar case—she didn't feel bad about it. Not as bad as she felt about admiring how good he looked with his damp hair curling at his neck, above an open-necked white shirt and blue jeans, and a cognac leather jacket almost the same colour as the one she'd stashed in Rowan's closet on arrival.

Rowan didn't wear such things. Which was why she'd raided her sister's wardrobe to put together an outfit for tonight.

When they'd been modelling, Rowan had always been the one to object to the more outlandish clothes, the ones people would never wear in the real world—but Willow had always suspected that secretly she loved them. It made it all feel more like dress-up, make-believe.

That was sort of how she'd felt, standing in front of the rail of Rowan's clothes, looking at all the colours and textures.

Willow had always been more of a neutral, classics girl. Simple basics showed off her beauty best, according to Ben, and countless other designers. But Rowan had stopped caring about that once she'd left the modelling world, it seemed. She wore the colours and the designs that appealed to her, that made her happy.

A memory surfaced, from a long London

summer years ago, when Rowan had been almost housebound by her own anxiety. She'd taught herself to make her own clothes—all so different from the outfits they modelled on the catwalk. These clothes weren't about making a statement, or being controversial, or even showing off as much skin as possible.

Rowan's clothes had been about comfort and love. She'd picked colours that vibrated happiness, styles and fabrics that swept around her like a protective cloak. They'd been amazing.

It was something she did, Willow had realised from her explorations of the cottage. She'd found a tiny sewing room in the back with an empty dress form, baskets full of material and pattern paper and her trusty sewing machine in the middle on a sturdy table. From the designs pinned up on the walls, she'd been making clothes for more than just herself too.

Willow didn't have that talent. But she *did* know how to put together an outfit. So she'd raided Rowan's wardrobe and settled on a long printed skirt in a Mediterranean blue, she suspected was one of her sister's creations, worn with a fitted sweater and her own boots. She considered for a moment before pulling out her own leather jacket too. If people didn't know

Rowan all that well, they might not know it wasn't her style either.

'Passably Rowanish,' Gwyn said now, as he stood in the doorway. 'Come on. We'll walk in. The night's mild enough.'

And it wasn't raining, which Willow always thought an unexpected but welcome bonus when at the British seaside.

They walked side by side down the hill towards the lights of the village ahead, and Willow found herself uncomfortably aware of the man beside her. Not just how good he looked in that jacket, or how much she wanted to touch that curl at his neck. The way his scent mingled with the salt of the sea, making it warmer, spicier. The way he laughed, warm but not mocking, when she made a comment about folk music and dancing to it in primary school.

'You might be surprised,' he told her. 'I suspect we're talking about a different sort of folk song.'

She hoped so. Those songs—all plinky strings and fake Ye Olde English—hadn't really been her sort of thing.

She took a deep breath, and got another lungful of that scent that was half Gwyn, half seaside. Why was she suddenly so aware of him? It couldn't just be damp hair and a jacket, could it?

Hormones, maybe. Pregnancy hormones were notoriously unpredictable, according to the websites she'd found. What else could have her lusting after her sister's grumpy neighbour on just a couple of days' acquaintance?

Hormones were responsible for that hug outside the doctor's surgery too. That damn hug. *That* was probably why she was so focused on his physical presence all of a sudden.

How long had it been since she'd been that close to another person? Probably the night her baby was conceived, actually. And even then...that had been sex, not closeness.

It felt wrong that she was only just now realising how different those two things were.

Damn, I have to learn a lot more about the world before I can be a mother.

But that hug...it had felt like closeness. It had felt—not intimate, exactly, but supportive. As if Gwyn had been sharing his strength and support with her, even though she'd been the one to throw herself into his arms.

It had almost felt like trust.

For someone she'd only known a few days, that was a lot.

The lights of the village grew brighter as

they reached the high street, meandering along to the square at the centre. And as they approached the Star and Dragon, Willow could already hear the strains of guitars and harmonising voices.

Gwyn was right; it didn't sound anything like the traditional folk music they'd danced to at primary school.

'Come on.' Gwyn picked up the pace a little as they crossed the square. 'Let's hope we can still get a table.'

Nobody even looked up as they crossed the threshold into the pub, the door swinging shut behind them. The crowd's focus was entirely on the two people on the stage—a young man with a guitar and a woman playing another, smaller stringed instrument. They both leaned in to sing into microphones, harmonising beautifully even as they played complex chords and melodies on both instruments.

Willow wouldn't claim to be an expert on music, but she knew about captivating a room—and these two had this room's attention all sewn up.

'They're good,' she murmured as Gwyn led her towards a free table at the back, near the bar.

'They are,' he agreed. 'That's my nephew Sean and his girlfriend Kayla.'

Willow glanced down at the guitar case he'd brought with him. 'I guess you're where he gets the talent from, then?'

'Mostly he's just worked damn hard at it.' Gwyn handed her a menu. 'What do you fancy? I can recommend the lasagne.'

The menu was standard pub fare—the lasagne came with chips—and Willow tried to remember the last time she'd ordered food like this anywhere. If she was out with Ben, they were usually in the sort of restaurants that required a tie. At home, she had a food delivery service that provided freshly prepared meals with the correct balance of all macros and micronutrients to keep her in shape.

For the first few weeks of her pregnancy, she'd mostly been concentrating on keeping food down. But as the weeks had passed, the nausea had receded, even as the fear had increased—and now, she suddenly realised, she was starving.

And she was eating for two.

She handed the menu back. 'Lasagne sounds great. With chips.'

He looked amused and as he brushed past her to get to the bar and order, he dipped his head until his mouth was right by her ear. 'Very good. Just what Rowan would have ordered.'

It wasn't until he'd gone that she remembered he'd told her Rowan never came here, so he was probably joking.

So she settled back against the wood panelling of the wall, let the music surround her and tried to fit in.

CHAPTER FIVE

IT WAS, Gwyn had to admit, pretty surreal standing at the familiar bar of the Star and Dragon, listening to the same conversations he heard here every week, with the soundtrack of Sean and Kayla's music, knowing that just over there sat Willow Freaking Harper, waiting for her lasagne.

His life had had odd moments before, but this was probably taking the biscuit.

It was good that there was a queue at the bar because he needed a few moments to make sense of it all in his head, anyway. He'd tried to process it in the shower before going to meet her, but his body kept remembering the feel of hers against him as she hugged him, and that wasn't helping at all, so he'd given up for the time being.

Yes, she was beautiful. But she was also pretending to be his friendly neighbour—who he'd definitely never had those sorts of thoughts about—and she would be leaving to go back to New York in a few short weeks.

Oh, yeah, and she was pregnant with another man's child.

So, really, he needed to get his mind out of any gutters.

To distract him, he focused in on the harmonies swirling around him. Sean and Kayla had moved on to another, more melancholy song—one about the sea and the tides and the passing of time and loss. It made his chest feel tight, but he had to admit the duo had nailed it. Sean had always been talented, but since meeting Kayla they'd taken things to another level.

They should be playing bigger gigs than the local folk night. They should be out there, making music.

He knew it, had known it for a while. But he pushed the thought away all the same.

At least here they were safe. Out there… Gwyn knew how tough it was. And how big the risks were if you wanted the real payoffs.

Not to mention everything you had to leave behind.

'Hello, stranger.' His sister Abigail hoisted herself up onto the bar stool beside him. 'I thought you weren't going to show tonight, and then your nephew would have been very disappointed. They're playing some new songs to-night.' She dropped her voice to a whisper. 'He's hoping to impress you.'

'He always impresses me,' Gwyn admitted. 'They're good, the pair of them. They're good together.'

'Remind you of anybody?' Abigail asked, too innocently.

'No.' Gwyn shut down the line of conversation with one syllable and a look, the way he always did when anyone tried to talk about Darrell. He'd have thought people would have learned by now.

Abigail sighed, and shifted her attention somewhere over his left shoulder. 'Is that your neighbour? The secret model?'

'Ex-model,' Gwyn corrected her. He knew Rowan was sensitive about her history, so people generally didn't bring it up in front of her—even if they discussed it behind her back. And since Willow was still determined to pretend to be Rowan, he might as well keep up the charade.

'Whatever.' Abigail waved her hand. 'You brought her here? I didn't know you two were going-out-together friends.'

Gwyn shrugged. 'We were chatting, and she was out of groceries, so I invited her to join me for dinner.' As the bartender finally reached him, he leant across to order their lasagnes, a pint for him and a lime and soda for Willow, as she'd requested.

When he leant back again, his sister was watching him even more sceptically. 'You know, that sounds surprisingly like a date.'

'It really doesn't.'

'Because you *don't* date,' Abigail replied with a nod. 'Does *she* know that?'

'She doesn't need to. Because this isn't a date.' He was almost certain that *Willow* didn't think it was a date. But then Willow had rather more information about the situation than his sister did. Like who she really was.

'Hmm.' Abigail still didn't look convinced. 'So, are you going to play for us tonight then? Grace us with your guitar up on the stage? Impress your not-a-date with your substantial…talent?'

He rolled his eyes as she elbowed him in the ribs. 'I brought my guitar. So…we'll see.'

He'd picked up his instrument out of habit rather than an actual intention to play. Sometimes he did, sometimes he didn't, but he always felt better knowing he had his own guitar at his side.

He never played the old songs, though—

Blackbird's songs, the ones people knew him for. He and Darrell had developed a reasonable following before his friend's death, and had a couple of breakout hits that people knew. But Gwyn couldn't—wouldn't—play them alone.

Instead, he'd moved away from the more rock styling they'd played together and over to a gentler, more folk-rock style, much like what Sean and Kayla were performing up on the stage. It seemed to fit his surroundings—and his mood—far better these days.

'It would be good to hear you play again.' Abigail's voice was softer now, and he almost missed the yearning in it. 'It's been a while.'

It had, Gwyn realised as he headed back to the table where Willow was waiting. It was probably the time of year. This season always reminded him of that terrible year when he'd lost Darrell, then returned to Rumbelow to find Abigail in trouble and Rachel—

Well. It held bad memories, was the point. He tended to get a little introverted around this time of year.

At least Willow arriving had distracted him from the usual doom spiral of his own thoughts.

She smiled up at him as he sat down beside her. 'Adoring fan?' When he looked confused, she nodded towards the bar where Abigail was still sitting, watching Sean play.

'My big sister, Abigail,' he explained. 'Sean's mum.'

Willow's eyebrows rose. 'She looks too young to have an almost grown-up son.'

'She had Sean young—she was only eighteen when she got married.' Willow didn't need the whole story, he figured. He didn't particularly want to tell it either.

'So she's, what? Thirty-something now?'

'Thirty-five,' he confirmed. 'There's a six-year age gap between us.'

Willow glanced back at Abigail. 'Well, she looks great.'

'I'll tell her you said so.' He wouldn't, he knew. Mostly because it would be weird telling his sister that.

Their lasagnes arrived just as Sean and Kayla stepped down from the stage. Folk night always took a similar format; someone would be booked to play for the first half of the evening, often Sean and Kayla these days, then the second half would be an open mic sort of affair, or floor night, as Ray, who ran it, called it.

There were a good number of musicians in the village and more travelled in from the surrounding area, so they were never short of performers. Tonight, they had a group of fishermen from two villages over, singing sea shanties, followed by three siblings on fiddle, cello and acoustic guitar.

At their secluded table they were still able to talk over the music, so they chatted while they ate—staying away from any contentious or deep topics, or anything that might give away Willow's identity to someone eavesdropping nearby. It made for a light, inconsequential, but surprisingly relaxing conversation. Gwyn hadn't expected her to be so easy to talk to.

Too easy, almost. More than once he found himself on the verge of saying something that he didn't mean to. Something about his past, and the people in it, that would lead to explanations and stories he didn't want to tell.

Not to mention the pity. There was always pity in people's eyes as they heard those stories for the first time. And he really didn't want to see it in hers.

He'd almost convinced himself that they'd get out of there and home without incident, when Sean and Kayla arrived beside the table.

'Are you going to play tonight, Gwyn?' Kayla asked. She was a sweet thing—petite and delicate, with a short, dark pixie cut and an infectious smile.

Willow turned to him with a smile that did things to his insides that Kayla's didn't. Things he was trying to ignore. 'Are you?'

'Go on, Uncle Gwyn.' Sean pulled up a chair from the next table and sat down, tugging Kayla onto his lap. 'You haven't played in weeks.'

'Months,' Kayla corrected.

'I've *never* heard you play,' Willow added. Which was true for her sister too, luckily. He suspected Rowan might have been to folk night once or twice without him really noticing, but he didn't play that often.

Up on the stage, Ray was waiting, microphone in hand, looking intently in their direction. Apparently, this was a stitch-up.

Gwyn sighed, and reached for his guitar case.

The pub fell silent as Gwyn took the stage, as if this was what they'd all been waiting for all night. Maybe it was.

Kayla slipped from Sean's lap into Gwyn's abandoned chair, resting her chin on her hand and her elbow on the table as she watched. Sean seemed equally rapt, waiting for his uncle to play.

Willow got the distinct impression she was missing something here.

Up on the stage, Gwyn settled himself onto a stool, his guitar across one knee, and plucked at a few strings, twisting pegs to get a better tuning. Then, into the waiting hush, he started to play.

And suddenly Willow knew *exactly* what she'd been missing, and wondered how it had been absent from her life for so long.

It wasn't just that he was *good*. He was captivating. Each note—not just strummed but plucked, making it sound like a hundred instruments were playing at once—rose up into the air and hung there like a perfume, changing the very feel of the pub. This wasn't an open mic night any more. It was a secret performance by a master, and everyone in the room felt it.

By the time he started to sing, Willow was already enraptured. His voice was low and warm, deeper somehow than his speaking voice, and she felt it behind her ribcage, vibrating through her bones. He sang of love and loss, of hope and disappointment—and most of all of carrying on, alone.

She didn't think she'd ever heard anything more beautiful, or more heartbreaking.

'He's good,' Willow murmured, making Kayla scoff.

'He's *great*,' she corrected.

'Sometimes I wonder if she's just dating me for my uncle,' Sean joked.

Kayla leaned into him and planted a soppy kiss on his cheek. 'Nah. Too much baggage for me.'

Willow didn't know what Gwyn's baggage was, but as she listened to him sing she knew she was hearing the effects of it. Whatever had happened in his past, it had changed him. And she got the feeling he still hadn't moved past it.

'What kind of baggage?' she asked.

Sean and Kayla exchanged a look. 'He never told you? About, well. Darrell, I guess.' Sean looked uncomfortable just saying the name.

'It's not a secret,' Kayla said quickly. 'I mean, it's all over the internet. It was in the news at the time. I'm surprised you don't already know.'

'I was probably still in the States,' Willow hedged, hoping that the timelines worked out for Rowan as well as her.

'Yeah, maybe it wasn't as big a story over there,' Sean allowed.

Willow swallowed a sigh of relief. 'Will you tell me? I mean, I could Google, but we all know how accurate that can be. And, well, I don't really like to ask Gwyn...'

'God, no.' Kayla's eyes went wide. 'He won't talk about it anyway. I mentioned it *once* and we didn't see him here for, like, a month.'

'That's what I'm worried about,' Willow said. 'We're just starting to hang out a little more now, and I don't want to put my foot in it.' All true, even if she hadn't explained the reasoning behind it. Those were *her* secrets, after all.

Okay, maybe it was rude to try and get Gwyn's secrets out of his nephew and his girlfriend. But it wasn't as if Gwyn didn't already know all of hers. She was just evening up the score.

Kayla looked to Sean, who shrugged. 'I guess there's no reason not to tell you,' he said. 'Maybe you can even convince him that it's time to move on.'

'Or to let *us* move on,' Kayla muttered, which Willow didn't quite understand, but hoped would make sense before long.

'Uncle Gwyn used to be in a band with his best friend, Darrell,' Sean said. 'They played around here a lot and made a name for themselves, then they moved up to London and started playing bigger gigs. They were spotted by some talent scout and, before they knew it, they were supporting some huge band or another on a European tour.'

'Wow. What were they called? Would I have heard of them?' Willow asked.

'Blackbird,' Kayla supplied. 'They had a couple of big hits on their own too. You'd probably know them if you heard them.'

Well, Willow knew what she *would* be tracking down on the internet when she got back to Rowan's cottage. If the songs he was playing tonight were any indication, she wanted to hear more.

But she also knew that this story wasn't going to have a happy ending. Gwyn's songs told her that much.

'What happened?' she asked. 'Where's Darrell now?' Had his best friend betrayed him? Run off with his girlfriend, maybe? Taken a solo contract and left Gwyn behind? Embezzled their money? Any of them sounded perfectly plausible.

But the serious look on Sean's face told her it was worse than that.

'He…he died. He got into drugs, hard and heavy, when they were touring and, well. Uncle Gwyn tried to help him, even got him into rehab, but it never stuck. And the last time…'

'He checked himself out and went straight to his dealer,' Kayla finished. 'Gwyn found his body the next day.'

'Oh, God.' Willow had seen a lot on the modelling circuit, and there were always recreational drugs around at the parties Ben dragged her to—not that she'd ever indulged, it wasn't her scene. But she'd never seen the way they could ravage a life like Gwyn had. 'That was when he came home to Rumbelow?'

Sean nodded. 'Seven years ago now. He was only, like, five years older than I am now, and he'd already quit the business. It's crazy.'

'He still writes though,' Kayla added. 'Music for other people—and some for himself, like this. But he never plays, except for at folk night here. And he never goes to any industry awards or events or anything, no matter how many times they invite him.'

From the tone of Kayla's voice, Willow surmised that the teenager was both baffled by and a little envious of this. Having been to enough similar sort of events herself, Willow could see both sides. They were always glamorous and fun, but they meant putting yourself on display—which was why Rowan had hated them, and modelling generally.

For Gwyn, knowing—or at least believing—that everyone looking at him would be seeing the ghost of his dead friend, she could understand such occasions would be unbearable.

'At least he still plays here,' she said softly, as the song Gwyn was singing drifted to a close. 'It would have been a travesty if he'd stopped playing altogether.'

'Agreed,' Sean said.

'What's agreed?' Gwyn's sister, Abigail, leant against the wall beside their table. 'Sean, Ray wants to know if you and Kayla will go back on after Gwyn finishes, to close the night?'

'Go on *after* Uncle Gwyn?' Sean shook his head. 'No, thanks.'

Kayla rolled her eyes. 'Of course we will,' she told Abigail, then turned to Sean. 'I know he's amazing, but he's also the old guard. You can't be intimidated by him all your life.'

'I'm not intimidated by him,' Sean objected. 'I *respect* him. That's different.'

'And that's fine, but when you start making life decisions based solely on what he thinks is a good idea—'

'I'm not—' Sean broke off as Gwyn, guitar back in its case, joined them at the table.

'You two up again now?' He motioned to his seat, and Kayla jumped up.

'We are.' Kayla grabbed Sean's hand and dragged him back towards the stage, Abigail trailing behind to watch.

Leaving Willow alone with Gwyn, and the twinge of guilt she felt for talking about him behind his back.

Gwyn hadn't caught much of the conversation between Willow and his family, but he'd heard enough.

He supposed it was only fair; he knew her secrets, so of course she wanted to know his. He'd just been enjoying spending time with her without seeing that look in her eye. The pitying look everyone gave him once they knew his story.

And if she'd got it from Sean and Kayla, she didn't even know the half of it.

'Making friends?' he asked mildly as he picked up his pint.

Willow winced. 'You heard what we were talking about?'

'Me, I'm guessing?' He was fairly sure he was the biggest bone of contention between his nephew and his girlfriend, given that Kayla wanted them to move to London and Sean was only saying no on his say-so.

'They were telling me why you don't play

music much any more. Or participate in the industry.' At least she wasn't trying to hide it. He got the feeling that Willow was usually upfront about things. Apart from her pregnancy, it seemed.

'All my dirty secrets, huh?'

She gave him a speculative look, as if she were seeing new angles to him she hadn't considered before. Perhaps she was. So far, their friendship had been weighted towards her problems. Maybe it was only just occurring to her that he might have some too.

'I don't think all of them,' she said after a pause. Then she shifted in her chair, turning back to look at Sean and Kayla on the stage. They were playing an old favourite, and plenty of people were clapping or singing along.

They really were too good to be stuck playing here.

'What did Kayla mean? When she said Sean was making life decisions based on what you thought?' Willow asked.

Oh, but he did *not* want to have this conversation tonight. Because that one question just led to a world of hurt he didn't want to revisit. Ever.

But Willow was waiting for an answer.

'She wants them to move to London. Look

for streets paved with gold, fame and fortune, that sort of thing.'

'And you don't want them to go?' Willow guessed.

'I think they're not ready. They're too young, too raw. The industry would chew them up and spit them out.' He knew he was right about this. And yeah, maybe he had his own reasons for not wanting them to go, but that didn't mean he was wrong. 'Abigail agrees.'

'I'm sure she does.' Willow's voice was mild, but he heard something else behind it.

'Want to say what you really mean?' He knew he sounded testy, but it was difficult to care. Just playing tonight had already got his emotions swirling, the way it always did. He loved to play—to perform. It was part of who he was. He knew he couldn't give it up entirely. But even just doing a few songs at folk night was usually enough to send him back to the bar for something stronger than beer. And more than one of them.

Tonight, though, he had to get Willow home safely, and that meant staying sober. It also made it a lot harder to avoid this conversation, and the feelings he'd been pushing down about it.

'Just that...if I was a mother, I'm sure I

wouldn't want my seventeen-year-old son running off to London with his girlfriend chasing an almost impossible dream either.' Her eyes widened as her own words obviously sank in. 'Oh, God. Not if. When.'

'Yeah. So you see my point.' He took another long glug of his pint and wondered if one whisky would be so bad. 'I'm just looking out for them.'

'Right. I mean, it's hard to crush the dreams of someone we love, but it's a competitive field. They might not be good enough.' She was watching him over the rim of her glass as she said it, and he knew that the righteous anger that rose up in him was exactly what she was trying to provoke.

Knowing that didn't stop him from reacting, though. 'Are your ears missing? Did you not hear them tonight? Of course they're good enough. They're incredible.'

'So why don't you want them to go?'

He didn't answer. How could he?

Willow sighed. 'Look. As someone who was on the public stage long before I finished school—and instead of finishing school actually—I get that it's problematic. There are definitely issues about being in that world too young, too naive and too inexperienced. It's not for everybody, that's for sure. Look at my sister! If our mother hadn't forced us to be the most famous, recognisable and lucrative versions of ourselves we could be, Rowan probably wouldn't have spent the last six years hiding out here. But the flip side of that is… if it's what they want, what they're made for, they're going to do it anyway. You have to let them make their own mistakes.'

'Even if it kills them?' The words shot out before he could stop them, and he was relieved when he looked around to see that everyone else in the pub was paying rapt attention only to Sean and Kayla on the stage.

'I understand why you're worried about that,' Willow said cautiously. 'And I won't say I didn't worry about it for Rowan at one point. That's why I helped her get out. She knew she wasn't alone. And maybe…maybe that's what they need too.'

She had a point, not that he was about to admit that. When he and Darrell had left, it had just been the two of them, out in the big wide world. Neither of them had been close to their parents, and Abigail… Well. She'd had her own problems back then.

He'd had Rachel, though, back in Rumbelow. Or he'd thought he did.

Turned out he'd had no one, same as Darrell. Maybe he was just lucky he hadn't ended up following the same path.

'They're seventeen,' he said bluntly. 'What they need is to stay home, finish their education, and figure out that there are no golden streets out there. You pay for everything you get in this life, and sometimes the price is far higher than the reward.'

'Is that what you learned?'

Gwyn drained the last of his pint and slammed the glass down on the table. 'Yep. Come on. Let's get you home.' And him back to his home, and the bottle of whisky he kept on the top shelf for the rare nights like this.

Before he had to talk about this with her any more.

CHAPTER SIX

IT WAS OVER a week before Willow spoke to Gwyn again.

Oh, she still saw him every day, jogging past her window, but even when she raised a hand to wave, he either didn't see her or ignored her.

She was guessing the latter.

Whether it was the conversation about his nephew at folk night, the fact that she now knew his secrets rather than him hoarding hers, or even the hug outside the doctor's clinic that had driven him away, she wasn't sure. But she was pretty much certain that he was avoiding her.

Maybe that was for the best. They'd only known each other a little over a week and had found themselves spilling secrets best kept hidden, and growing closer than was strictly advisable, given that she was pregnant and in hiding from the father, and he was potentially her sister's only friend in her hideaway town. Not to mention that she'd be leaving soon.

No point spending time getting closer, under those circumstances.

But that didn't mean she could completely ignore the little pang in her chest every time he ran past without seeing her.

Still, she tried.

Her grocery shop was delivered, and she busied herself putting that away—and reorganising Rowan's kitchen cupboards while she was at it. She hunted through the cottage for clues as to her sister's state of mind, and what she'd been up to for the last six years that hadn't made it into their regular video chats. She admired the dress designs stuck up on the walls, and wondered at all the talent Rowan was hiding away here in the little Cornish village.

When that grew boring, she took to the beach. It was still too early in the year for it to be packed with tourists, although there were a few surfers out, and the usual dog walkers. She needed to stay active, but she wasn't sure exactly what was safe to do, or what would bring the nausea back, so she stuck to walking for now.

And while she walked, she thought. Mostly in circles, but she had to start somewhere.

She thought about Ben. About the kind of

mother she wanted to be. She tried to picture her life in a year, in three years, in ten. She used every goal and visualisation trick she'd ever learned from any guru or therapist.

And she ended up right where she'd started. Hiding out pretending to be her sister, unable to fully picture a life in which she was a mother and doing it right.

Or one in which she was able to stand up to Ben and tell him what she wanted.

That was the most frustrating part. Nobody who knew her would call Willow Harper a pushover, or weak, or needy—but Ben made her feel like all three. When he was in a room, it felt as if he sucked all the air—or power—out if it. As if nothing she could do or say mattered when he was there.

When they'd first met, he'd loved that she was beautiful, and a model, and in demand. It was what had attracted him to her—she knew that, because he'd told her as much.

But as their relationship—such as it was—had developed, he'd started complaining about her showing too much skin in campaigns, or wearing 'inappropriate' dresses to events. Where before he'd wanted everyone to admire her, lately he seemed to have decided that he wanted her all to himself. He even complained if she spoke too long to anyone else at parties—especially other men, even if they'd been friends for years.

The last six months or so, she'd got the feeling she couldn't do anything right. That just who she *was* wasn't enough. But at the same time, Ben had been getting closer, clingier. Intimating that it was time to take their relationship/business arrangement to the next level. He'd been using words like 'logical conclusion' and 'plays well on paper', none of which was entirely convincing, or at all romantic.

But maybe she shouldn't be looking for romantic. She was pregnant. She was going to be a mother. Maybe she needed to be looking at the practical side of things instead.

When that day's walk reached its usual inconclusive conclusion, she sighed and decided that coffee would help. Even decaf.

She trudged up the path from the beach into the village rather than turning back towards the steep steps that led up to her cottage. This way, she could have a sit and ruminate some more before she walked the shallower but longer path home. Maybe she'd even bump into Gwyn on one of his runs.

And she was back to thinking about Gwyn again. Great.

She pushed him from her mind and focused on her surroundings instead. Rowan said she found this place grounding, settling. Maybe that was what she needed to find here too.

Spring had definitely arrived in Rumbelow, and the sun actually felt warm at last. Blue skies shone overhead, decorated with wispy white clouds bouncing past on a fresh, but not cold, breeze. Box planters on the sides of the road were blooming with spring bulbs—tulips and daffodils and other flowers she couldn't even identify brightened up the pathways everywhere she walked. Shops had windows and doors open for the first time since she'd arrived, and the scent of baking bread was enticing.

Babies needed carbs, right? Just because *she* didn't usually eat them…right now, she wasn't just eating for her. Finding somewhere to serve her a decaf coffee and some hot buttered toast was basically a moral obligation at this point. Ooh, and maybe some eggs. Or even a sausage sandwich…

She skipped the café where she'd bumped into Gwyn the other morning, more because it was Rowan's local than because she was worried she might see him again and it would be awkward. Rumbelow had a surplus of lovely-looking independent cafés to enjoy, and it seemed wrong to stick to just one of them. Plus, she didn't fancy getting served tea she didn't want again.

With her depressingly decaf coffee and a sausage bap, she took a small table for two in the corner and watched the world go by for a while.

Until Gwyn's sister walked in and waved as she headed for the queue.

Willow stared down at her almost empty coffee cup and debated her options. She could drain it and run, before Abigail was able to get her own drink and join her. Or she could stay here and connect with Gwyn's sister—and maybe learn a little more about the man himself.

Put like that, it was an easy decision.

When Abigail made a beeline for her table with two coffee cups in hand, Willow knew it was the right one. This was a woman who understood early morning needs.

'Decaf, yeah?' she said, taking a seat. 'That's what Shelley at the counter said you were drinking.'

'Yeah, thanks.' Willow tried a friendly smile. It didn't feel so bad. 'It felt like a coffee sort of morning, but I don't want to get all jangly, you know?' No need to explain about caffeine being bad for the baby no one but Gwyn knew about yet.

'I'm glad I caught you, actually.' Abigail blew across the surface of her coffee, holding the cup gently between two hands. 'I've been meaning to talk to you.'

Willow's smile froze just a little bit. In her experience, those words meant what was about to follow could really go either way—but it was usually one extreme or another.

Gwyn's sister was shorter than he was by a whole head, and curvier by far, but she had the same dark hair and eyes. When she pinned her with her—not unfriendly but certainly determined—gaze across the café table, Willow knew that she probably should have run.

'Oh?' she said, trying to portray mild curiosity rather than fear. She took a sip from her fresh coffee and pretended it had caffeine in it.

'Yes. I wanted to say how glad I am that you and Gwyn have become…closer lately.'

'Closer friends,' Willow said quickly. 'Just… closer *friends*.'

Abigail's smile was far too knowing. Even if what she thought she knew was wildly inaccurate. 'Of course. It's just that Gwyn hasn't had so many friends around here since he came home. He doesn't tend to let people in and, well, it's just nice to see him opening up a little.'

'He's been a very good friend to me,' Willow said sincerely. Maybe with just a little extra emphasis on the word *friend,* just in case.

'I'm sure you have to him too.' Abigail smiled brightly over her coffee cup. 'That's why I wanted to ask you to join us for Sunday dinner tomorrow. If you're not too busy?'

Every conceivable excuse to get out of it flew from Willow's mind, leaving it utterly blank. 'Um... I...' She hesitated, then sighed. Really, a home-cooked meal sounded glorious. She wasn't much of a cook herself, and cooking for one was boring, so her grocery delivery had mostly been easy to assemble, simple meals. Besides, it had been a long time since she'd had a proper English Sunday roast. Gwyn might not like it, but at least he wouldn't be able to avoid her any longer.

'That would be lovely,' she said, more firmly. 'What can I bring?'

'You invited *who*?' Obviously, Gwyn had to be imagining things, because there was no way that his sister could possibly have said what he thought she'd said.

'I invited Rowan over for Sunday lunch this

afternoon,' Abigail repeated calmly, as if the words meant nothing.

Of course, if she had *really* invited Rowan, they wouldn't, much. He could have been pleasant and friendly and then she'd have gone away again and he could have relaxed with his family. It would have been fine.

But Rowan was in New York, pretending to be Willow. Which meant that Abigail had *actually* invited world-famous supermodel Willow Harper for roast beef and Yorkshire puddings.

The same Willow he was actively trying to avoid right now.

Looked like that plan was out of the window.

He ran a hand through his hair and sighed. 'I thought it was going to be just us. I *thought* we were going to talk to Sean and Kayla again about, well, you know.'

'We can't talk about London—the capital city of our country—with another person in the house?' Abigail's eyebrows were raised ludicrously high.

'You're being annoyingly disingenuous,' he told her. 'Stop it.'

His sister flashed him a smile. 'Honestly, Gwyn, I didn't think it was a problem. Sean and Kayla adored her the other night, and everyone knows the two of you have been spending time together lately—'

'No, we haven't.' Not that week, anyway. Not since the folk night.

Abigail's expression was quintessential Long-Suffering Big Sister. 'Gwyn, you brought her to folk night. And just because you drove out the long way, don't think nobody spotted you and her sneaking out together in your car last week either.'

Damn. As long as whichever busybody who'd seen them hadn't followed them to the midwife's appointment, they were probably okay, though.

Gwyn really wasn't sure how long Willow was going to be able to keep her identity— or her secret—between just the two of them. But he was pretty sure spending time with his sister and nephew would bring that timescale down considerably.

Abigail put her hand on his arm. 'Nobody's teasing you, Gwyn, or judging you either. Nobody who has noticed thinks this is a bad thing. People around here care about you, and they want you to be happy. If Rowan makes you happy, there's no reason to hide that, is there? You're *allowed* to be happy again, you know. Even after everything.'

Did he know that? Gwyn wasn't sure.

It was that 'everything' that was the problem. So much had happened, there'd already been so much loss, he wasn't sure he even knew how to *feel* happiness any more, let alone believe he deserved it.

Contentment was enough for him these days. And since that was a hell of a lot more than he'd ever expected to feel again when he'd first moved home, he saw no reason to rock that boat.

Besides, in his experience, when you rode a happiness high, it only meant you had further to fall.

The doorbell rang, and Gwyn cast a last glare at his sister before going to answer it.

Willow stood on the doorstep, a bunch of flowers and a bottle of wine in her hands, and an apprehensive look on her face.

'You didn't have to say yes,' he told her.

Willow shrugged. 'I have a weakness for roast beef.'

Abigail did make an excellent Sunday roast; he had to admit that much.

Gwyn stood aside to let her in and took the wine and flowers as she slipped her jacket from her shoulders. Underneath, she wore a simple black sweater and jeans, with a gold necklace and earrings, and he knew in a moment that Rowan would never be seen in something so plain.

Hopefully, his sister *didn't* know that.

'Am I underdressed for the occasion?' Damn. She'd caught him staring.

'You look fine,' he replied. And it was true. If fine also meant untouchable, beautiful, and the sort of woman it was hard to look at for too long without being blinded by the glow.

Yes, she was the most beautiful woman he'd ever seen, and his fingers itched to stroke along her cheek, her jaw and down her neck, just to feel her respond. That didn't mean he had to *tell* her that.

'Rowan! You're here!' Abigail emerged from the kitchen, looking slightly flustered and red in the face, her floral apron wrapped twice around her waist. 'Ooh, are those for me?' She held out a hand and Gwyn thrust the flowers into it. 'Nobody ever brings me flowers. Thank you! Come on through to the kitchen and we'll open that bottle of wine.'

Abigail turned to bustle back kitchenwards, and Gwyn gave Willow a knowing look.

Problem number one: bringing wine and then having to explain why she couldn't drink any, without letting on that she was pregnant, and lying about her identity.

She really hadn't thought this through, had she?

'I'm glad you like the flowers,' Willow said smoothly as she followed Abigail, leaving Gwyn to trail behind after completely ignoring his look. She swung a bag off her shoulder and pulled out another bottle. 'Actually, I brought some non-alcoholic stuff for myself, if you don't mind. I'm not drinking at the moment. Antibiotics.'

Of course. The classic antibiotics excuse. No one could question that. Why hadn't *he* thought of it?

Because he was in a complete mess about her being here in the first place, he admitted to himself finally.

He sank into a wooden chair at the kitchen table as the thought settled into his brain.

Watching her joking and laughing with Abigail made it feel like she was part of his life—in a way he didn't let himself experience any more. He didn't bring women home, he didn't make new friends, he didn't let new people into his life.

The people he already had to care for were more than enough trouble as it was.

Abigail. Sean. Himself, because that was sort of essential.

That was it. That was the list of people he cared about and looked after. Not because he hated everyone else, but because he already knew that three people was more than he could hope to keep safe.

He'd failed enough people in his life to not want to risk letting down any more. Abigail and Sean—they were already there, his family, and he loved them despite himself. The two of them, he'd accepted, he'd always do his best for—even if he knew he'd never let them see quite how much he worried about ruining things with them or for them. Abigail had already forgiven him for abandoning her once, for letting her get hurt. He never wanted to have to ask for that forgiveness again.

But he couldn't let more people in. No matter how appealing it was to play the knight in shining armour for Willow. She didn't actually *need* him to do it, he knew—and that helped, a bit. She had the strength, the brains and the money to be able to cope in this world perfectly well on her own.

Knowing that didn't seem to make it any easier for him to resolve to walk away and leave her to fix her own problems, though. Especially since she was currently taste-testing gravy in his sister's kitchen.

He *couldn't* let Willow in. He didn't have the capacity to worry about saving her as well as Abigail and Sean. Because she might not need him, exactly, but that didn't mean he couldn't help. Make a difference.

And that was all it could be, of course—helping her in her time of need. Because once that time of need was over, she'd be back to America in a flash. Maybe even back with the loser boyfriend/father of her child she'd run away from in the first place.

Gwyn had made a conscious effort not to Google her and find out who that man might be. He told himself that was because it was none of his business. And if part of his brain whispered that it was because he didn't want to see her with another man…well, he was ignoring that stupid part right now.

What did it matter to him who Willow dated? She was barely even a friend—and that only against his better judgement. Why would he feel *anything* at the idea of her dating someone, being with someone, having a baby with someone who wasn't him?

He swore silently inside his head. Denial

really wasn't going as well as he'd hoped it would.

'Why are you looking so down in the dumps over there?' Abigail asked over her shoulder, wooden spoon still in one hand.

Gwyn looked up to see Willow watching him curiously too. Her blue eyes were a little too knowing, for all the curiosity, though. As if she suspected the truth and was just waiting for him to admit it.

He'd already let her in, far more than he'd intended to when they'd met.

And a large part of him—one inconveniently located in his heart, he suspected—wanted to let her in even more.

To Willow's surprise, Sunday lunch with Gwyn's family was…lovely.

She'd been nervous about it ever since Abigail had invited her, second-guessing her decision to say yes, and that uncertainty had solidified in her stomach when she'd seen Gwyn's expression as he'd answered the door.

He didn't want her there, that much was patently obvious. And when Abigail had offered her a glass of wine she could see exactly why.

This was too much of a risk. Spending time with other people—kind, nice people who would expect her to be open and chatty and honest about her own life and things like, well, her identity—only increased the chances that someone would notice she wasn't who she said she was.

She'd almost turned around and left right then. But the look on Gwyn's face—as if he was just waiting for her to turn tail and run—had made her forge on, if only for the satisfaction of proving him wrong. And after Abigail bought her excuse about antibiotics, everything else ran surprisingly smoothly.

'That was delicious,' she told her hostess, pushing away her empty plate, with only a drizzle of gravy remaining to show that it had ever been piled high with roast beef, Yorkshire puddings, roast potatoes, vegetables and gravy. 'It was so kind of you to invite me.'

'Oh, we're not done yet,' Sean said. 'You haven't seen pudding. I mean, Mum's a great cook, but her desserts are to die for.'

Sean and Kayla hadn't seemed surprised to see Willow joining them at the Sunday dinner table, so she assumed Abigail had warned them they'd have company. More unusually, though, the addition of a stranger hadn't seemed to inhibit family conversation and discussion one bit. Friendly debate, rivalry and mocking had continued apace—almost as if Willow belonged there all along.

'Rowan never came for dinner at your sister's, did she?' she asked later, after they'd said their goodbyes and were heading back up the hill towards the cottage and Gwyn's lifeboat station—rather more slowly than she'd walked down. Abigail's desserts were, indeed, spectacular—and very filling.

'God, no,' Gwyn said. 'Abigail hardly ever invites anyone any more. When I first moved home, she was forever asking single friends and acquaintances along, trying to set me up with them. I put my foot down in the end, told her I wouldn't come at all unless she stopped inviting other people. It's family Sunday lunch, after all. It's only meant for family.'

Willow winced. 'I'm sorry. I didn't realise you felt so strongly about it.' That must have been why he'd looked so grumpy when she arrived.

But Gwyn flashed her a grin. 'Nah. I just said that to stop her matchmaking. It was…it was nice to have you there today.'

The unexpected compliment filled her with a warmth that the cool spring air didn't. 'It was nice to be invited. Your sister's a fantastic cook.'

'She is. So, you were just there for the food, then?'

'The company wasn't so bad either,' she admitted. 'Once you stopped sulking about me being there.'

'I wasn't sulking,' Gwyn said, even though he clearly had been. 'I just…' He sighed. 'I don't want them getting the wrong idea. About me and you.'

Ah. Of course. Suddenly the whole afternoon made a lot more sense.

'You're worried they might think we're more than friends?' she asked.

'Oh, I'm not worried they might,' he replied. 'I know they already do.'

Willow winced. 'Did Abigail say something to you?'

'She didn't have to. I could tell by the self-satisfied gleam in her eye. Like she had something to do with facilitating this imaginary relationship in the first place.'

He sounded more exasperated than angry, which Willow took as a good sign.

They walked in silence for a few more minutes, slowly winding their way along the climbing cliff path that led to Rowan's cottage. Willow had enough leftovers in her bag—thrust upon her by Abigail as they'd tried to leave—that she wouldn't have to go shopping for at least another day or so. Maybe she could just hibernate in the cottage until she figured out what to do next. That would solve the problem of people thinking she was dating Gwyn, at least.

Not any of her other problems, but then they were rather bigger things to deal with.

'It's not like I'm embarrassed or anything,' Gwyn said suddenly. 'Obviously, any guy would be thrilled to have people think he was dating you, or Rowan, for that matter.'

'If it's so obvious, then why are you pulling that face?' Willow couldn't help but ask. He looked physically pained at the idea of anyone thinking he was dating her, despite his words. 'Is it because I'm pregnant?'

Gwyn scoffed at that idea. 'No. It's not that—it's not you. It's—'

'Oh, not the "it's not you, it's me" speech!' Willow rolled her eyes dramatically. 'Didn't that go out *decades* ago?' She was teasing him, mostly. He couldn't exactly give her that breakup speech if they weren't dating—weren't *anything*—to begin with. But she meant it a little bit too. Obviously, there was something about her that made the idea of people thinking they were dating utterly repellent to him.

'It *is* me,' Gwyn said firmly. 'I don't date. I don't *want* to date. And I *definitely* don't want my family to get the idea that the situation around me dating is going to change any time soon. Or ever.'

'Oh.' Well, that really *was* him, not her. She supposed that was something. 'Why not?'

'Why not let them get the wrong idea?'

'No, of course not. I understand that. I meant…and this is not to be taken as a suggestion or an offer or anything more than a friendly question, okay?' She waited for his nod of agreement before she continued. 'Why don't you date?'

CHAPTER SEVEN

SHE LIKELY HADN'T meant her question to be such a stumper, but it still took Gwyn a good few moments to piece together an answer. Not because he didn't *know* the answer, but because he wasn't quite sure how much of it he wanted to share with her right now.

He could just say *bad experiences* and leave it at that. Or claim he was focusing on other areas of his life at present. Or invent some lost love he'd never got over—even if that one wasn't *entirely* invention.

Or, he supposed, he could tell her the truth.

'My last serious relationship…it ended badly. Very badly.' Maybe she'd just take that and leave it there, if he was lucky.

Except he'd never been that lucky.

'Can I ask what happened?' She didn't look at him as she asked the question, instead looking out over the cliffs to the sea. It gave him the space to consider his answer, which he appreciated.

He could lie. She'd never know the difference.

But he didn't.

'Sean and Kayla…they told you what happened with Darrell when we moved to London, right?'

Willow nodded. 'Sounds like you were on the verge of being the next big thing when he died.'

'Yeah. We were.' That had been something else to throw into the mix of grief and misery and guilt and loss he'd felt in the aftermath of finding Darrell's body. The loss of the future they were supposed to have together.

But that wasn't the only future he'd lost.

He took a deep breath. 'I'm guessing they didn't tell you about Rachel?'

'Rachel?' Her eyebrows jumped as she looked at him again. 'No. They didn't.'

'I'm pretty sure they don't even know the whole story,' he admitted. 'Almost nobody does, except Abigail and, well, Rachel herself. So I'd appreciate it if you didn't spread it around.'

'I wouldn't.' Willow focused her gaze on him, her blue eyes bright, wide and honest even in the falling gloom of the evening. 'You don't have to tell me, though, if you're worried.'

'I'm not.' It was true, as far as it went. He wasn't concerned that Willow would gossip about him—he held enough of her secrets to make keeping his a no-brainer.

If he was worried at all, it was only about how she'd react. How she'd look at him, after she knew.

'Okay,' she said. 'Then tell me. What happened with Rachel?'

Gwyn shoved his hands in his pockets as they walked, and tried to find the right way to start the story.

'Rachel and I…we were high school sweethearts. You know, the whole ridiculous made for each other thing. We thought—I thought—we were endgame.'

'But she didn't?' Willow guessed.

'She said she did.' It still hurt, remembering, even after all these years. 'She was still studying when Darrell and I moved to London, so she didn't come with us. Looking back, it's fairly obvious she didn't want to. That wasn't the kind of future she saw for herself. I guess… she liked having a boyfriend in a band when we were in school, but she always figured I'd give it up and get a real job eventually. I just didn't see that at the time.'

'So you went to London thinking she'd be waiting patiently at home for you…?'

'And she was, for a bit,' Gwyn replied. He knew already which way Willow's mind had gone, making Rachel the villain. And she wasn't entirely wrong. She just wasn't totally right either. 'I kept thinking she'd join us in London eventually, even when she got a job here after she finished studying. Which probably should have been a clue.'

Up ahead, Rowan's cottage gleamed pearly-white in the moonlight, the outside lamp glowing faintly. They were nearly home. Time to rip off the sticking plaster and tell the worst part of the story.

'Then she found out she was pregnant.' He felt Willow's grip on his arm tighten at the words. 'And she didn't tell me.'

'The baby was yours?' Willow asked. 'Sorry, not to cast aspersions or anything, but I don't know this woman.'

Turned out, neither had he. Not as well as he'd thought.

'It was mine,' he said tightly.

Willow was silent for a long moment. He wondered what she was thinking. If she thought he was judging her for not telling the father of her child yet. She didn't know that he'd completely understood Rachel's reasons. That was what made it even worse.

'Did she…did she keep it?' The tentativeness in her voice told him she'd jumped to the wrong conclusion, maybe inevitably. He'd never mentioned being a father or having a child, of course. Because he wasn't and he didn't.

Couldn't imagine he ever would, now.

'She found someone who could give her what she wanted,' he said, because he had to start there and work up to the rest. 'I don't know if it started before she knew about the baby or after, but it was certainly before she told me she was pregnant. The timings…the baby had to be mine. But she never had any intention of letting me raise it with her. I wasn't… I wasn't the sort of guy she imagined settling down with, apparently.'

The worst thing was, he couldn't even disagree with her.

Even before everything that happened with Darrell, he'd hardly been husband material, let alone *father* material. He'd been focused on his music career, and if that had gone as well as they'd hoped he'd have been touring most of the year. Yeah, other musicians did it, but he didn't think he could have—trying to concentrate on the music when worrying about a wife and a kid at home. He didn't have it in him.

And then, after Darrell…he'd known he couldn't risk it. Couldn't risk letting down someone else the way he'd let down his best friend—especially not letting down his own child. He couldn't save, protect or take care of anyone, and he wouldn't subject a kid to that.

He couldn't let more people in because he was already at maximum capacity for caring, and he couldn't take the consequences if he tried for more and failed. It was as simple as that. He wasn't built for relationships.

He didn't know if Willow would understand that, though. So instead, he said, 'She miscarried, just before the twelve weeks scan. After that…she didn't want to see me. She moved away with her new man and the last I heard they were happily married with three kids. She got what she wanted in the end.' And he was happy for her, really he was.

'But *you* didn't,' Willow said softly.

Gwyn shook his head. 'I never really saw myself as father material anyway.'

But the look Willow gave him told him she saw the deeper truth: he'd wanted to be. Just for that split second when she'd told him about the baby…he'd wanted to be good enough to have that.

But with Darrell's body still fresh in his mind, he'd known he never could be.

And now…now he couldn't afford to care that much. About anybody.

He'd worked so hard to try and keep Darrell safe and with them—and he'd let down Rachel because of it. Not just Rachel—Abigail and Sean too, not that they saw it that way.

He did.

He'd spread himself too thin, that was the problem. He had to prioritise. He couldn't afford another distraction—however needy, deserving, blonde or beautiful.

Even if she felt like a friend already. Someone who could understand him down to his bones.

So he pulled his arm away from hers as they reached her cottage. 'Here we are. Home safe.'

'Thank you.' Willow gave him a wry smile. 'Although I hardly think that Rumbelow is the sort of place where I need a bodyguard to get home on a Sunday evening.'

'Perhaps not. But we're a full-service sort of village.' The temptation to linger, to joke and banter—to accept the invitation for a last coffee that he was almost certain was about to be forthcoming—was huge. So he forced himself to turn away—to reach for the gate and open it, to *leave*.

Until a soft touch on his arm stopped him.

He huffed out a short, resigned sigh and turned back. 'You okay?'

Willow chewed on her lower lip, and he couldn't help but stare at her mouth. To imagine claiming it with his own. To picture taking her inside that cottage and kissing her again. With intent.

Because she'd felt like she belonged, this afternoon at family lunch. Just for those few hours, having her there had felt like what his life could have been, should have been.

But it was too late now.

'I was going to ask…but I will completely understand if you don't want to…' Willow paused, took a deep breath and started again. 'I've got my first scan at the hospital on Wednesday.'

'And you need me to take you?' Of course. Everyone needed something, and nobody ever seemed to understand that he didn't feel equipped to give it.

Willow shook her head. 'No. I can take a cab. I'm perfectly capable of going alone. But

I wondered… I wondered if you might *want* to come with me.'

'Why?'

Her smile was soft and gentle. 'Because you've been there for me since the moment I arrived here. I figured…you might want to see what it was all for.'

Gwyn wasn't prepared for the surge of emotions that flooded his senses. He tightened his jaw against them and gave a sharp nod. 'Wednesday, then.' Then he turned and walked away, towards his own sanctuary in the lifeboat station.

It was that or kiss her. And that would be a step too far down the road to certain disaster.

Wednesday came almost too quickly and too slowly at the same time.

On the one hand, Willow was terrified—about seeing her baby on the ultrasound screen and everything becoming real at last, and having to make a lot of decisions very quickly. On the other, she was impatient—to see her child, yes. And, if she was completely honest with herself, to see Gwyn.

He'd been avoiding her again since Sunday—since they'd shared that strange moment on her doorstep where he gave up some more of his secrets, mostly willingly, and when, just for a moment, she almost imagined he was about to kiss her.

Which was ridiculous, of course.

Gwyn had been nothing but a supportive friend to her, and that was only because of his friendship with her sister, she was sure. Not to mention the fact that she was pregnant with another man's child, and due to fly back to New York any time now.

Of course he hadn't been about to kiss her.

Even if, in the moment, she'd really wanted him to.

With a sigh, she threw herself back into the kitchen chair to finish the dregs of her tea and wait for Gwyn to pick her up.

It had to be the hormones again, didn't it? Because as gorgeous as Gwyn was—she was pregnant, not blind—she was under no illusions that starting something romantic between them would be a disaster. For both of them. Quite aside from her current, rather complicated, situation, he obviously had a lot of past trauma he still needed to work through, and she had no intention of trying to fix anybody. Not when she was still pretty broken herself, if she was honest.

Her relationship with Ben, such as it was,

had been exposed in the aftermath of her pregnancy test as nothing more than a sham. A show for the cameras. It wasn't real love, or support, or respect, or any of those other things she knew a relationship needed to be.

Ironically, she was pretty sure that Gwyn *could* give those things—if not to her, then to someone—but he was too scared now to let himself.

She sighed again into her teacup. Maybe that was why they got along so well. They were both a mess, in their own particular way, and neither of them expected the other to be anything but.

Willow looked around the cottage her sister had run away to all those years ago, and understood fully, maybe for the first time, the impulse that had led Rowan to hole up here. It wasn't just the beautiful views, the picturesque village or even the remote location.

It was the safety.

Here, halfway up a cliff, with her nearest neighbour a grumpy ex-musician in hiding, Rowan knew that she was safe from anyone who cared about who she had been before. Here, she could hide out, build a chrysalis around herself and wait until she was ready to emerge as a butterfly. As the person she wanted to be—away from the cameras and their mother's influence.

The only thing with Rowan was, given the chance, Willow suspected she'd have stayed wrapped up in that chrysalis for ever, just to avoid finding out what life looked like on the other side.

Which was just one of the reasons Willow had given her that push, out to New York, to find out what colour her wings were.

Willow, of course, didn't have the option of staying hidden for ever.

She had a baby inside her who'd be coming out in a matter of months, however scared she was, however uncertain about what life looked like on the other side. So she'd just have to woman up and find out.

And as if she'd needed a reminder of that, her jeans wouldn't fasten up this morning, and the maternity bras she'd ordered were already digging in. She'd had to place an emergency order for the next size up—and steal Rowan's jeans from the wardrobe, glad that her sister preferred to wear her clothes looser these days. The difference was hopefully barely noticeable to anyone else, but a godsend to her expanding middle.

She heard Gwyn's car crunch to a halt outside her gate and got to her feet, grabbing her bag and heading out to meet him before he made it to the door. He had his hand already raised to knock as she opened it.

'You ready?' He didn't meet her gaze exactly, ducking his head at first then looking over her shoulder, as if he was avoiding any unnecessary contact with her. When he took her bag, his fingers didn't brush hers. And when he opened the car door for her, he stepped back as far as he could before she climbed in.

Neither of them spoke until they were on the main road, speeding away from Rumbelow.

'So, what happens at this scan, then?' Gwyn asked. 'Will they tell you if it's a boy or a girl?'

'I'm not sure,' Willow admitted. 'I think usually at twelve week scans it's too early to tell. But I'm a little late having mine, so you never know.' At least three weeks late, if she was totally honest. She was pretty sure she'd been around twelve weeks already when she'd arrived in Britain, and it had taken a little while to get an appointment for the scan.

'So this is just to…check everything is okay?' There was an apprehension in Gwyn's voice that made her think of the story he'd told her the other day. Of the girl he'd left behind, and the baby they'd lost.

She shouldn't have asked him to come. This wasn't fair.

'You can wait in the car when we get there, you know,' she said. 'I don't need you to come in with me.'

'Maybe I want to.' He didn't look at her as he said it, though.

'Why?' She realised the answer as soon as she asked the question. 'Never mind.'

He was coming in with her in case there was a problem. He didn't want her to be alone if the scan showed up something…bad.

She reached out and squeezed his hand where it sat on the gear stick. 'Thank you.'

The hospital was bigger and whiter than the doctor's surgery where she'd visited the midwife. Given the distance they'd had to drive to get there, Willow suspected it must service a large proportion of the county of Cornwall.

Gwyn parked the car after circling the car park for a short while, then they headed in together.

Willow had never spent much time in hospitals in her life, but it seemed that Gwyn had a better idea of where they needed to be, so she followed him.

'You know your way around this place pretty well,' she said as she trotted after him.

'There are signs.' He pointed his chin up towards the overhead signs, his jaw still tight and his face closed off.

'Right. Of course.'

Luckily, they didn't have to spend too long in the sterile waiting room, once they found it. Just long enough for her to flip through all the pregnancy and baby magazines on the table, and for him to stare stonily at the wall. Willow sneaked glances at the other couples going into the ultrasound room—mostly looking excitedly nervous—and the ones coming out again, looking slightly stunned.

It's just a scan. Just a picture. As long as everything is okay, this will be over and done with and I can keep moving on. It's just a scan.

Except it wasn't, not really.

It was concrete proof—in a way that the sickness or her aching boobs or even the eight positive tests she'd taken hadn't been—that she was growing a new life inside her.

She reached over and grabbed Gwyn's hand, just as the nurse called her name.

'And this must be dad,' the ultrasound technician said as she motioned for Willow to get comfortable in the chair.

'Not exactly,' Gwyn said drily. 'I'm just here for moral support.'

'He's a friend,' Willow explained. 'The father is…overseas at the moment. On business.'

'Right.' The technician looked between them with a slightly knowing smile, but didn't say anything more. Willow supposed she must see all sorts of couples and parental setups in her job. It wouldn't do if she passed judgement on them all.

Besides, it wasn't as if Willow had anything to apologise for here. She hadn't searched the internet for evidence of what Ben was up to in her absence, but she would place money that it was more scandalous than hospital appointments with a friend, or folk nights and Sunday dinners.

The technician got Willow to raise her top and lower the waistband of her leggings, at which point Gwyn started pointedly studying the posters on the walls about smoking and drinking during pregnancy, amongst other things.

'Let's see what we've got in here, shall we?'

The gel was cold on her belly and her core muscles tightened even more—and every muscle she possessed already felt taut with expectation and fear. Willow swallowed and reached out, groping blindly for something, anything to hold on to for reassurance.

She felt Gwyn's fingers tighten around hers in response, and smiled.

Gwyn hated hospitals. He'd hated hospitals for far longer than he could justify from the disasters of the last decade of his life. He'd hated them when he'd visited his grandparents in the last years of their respective lives. He'd hated them when he'd visited Abigail after she had Sean. And he'd hated them more recently too, for more obvious reasons.

Maybe it was the smell as much as the memory. The whiff of death that filled the place. And the people sitting around, tense, waiting for bad news, knowing that life as they knew it could be about to change in just a fraction of a second, in just one or two words.

He definitely knew how that felt.

But Willow had asked him to be there, and it wasn't as if she had anybody else right now, and so...here he was.

He'd reasoned it out to himself as he'd lain awake in bed the night before.

He'd promised himself he wouldn't let anyone else in, that he wouldn't open himself up to letting down and losing another person—Abigail and Sean were enough. But Willow wasn't staying; she wouldn't be here long enough for him to let her down, and losing her was inevitable anyway, so he wouldn't let himself get too close. He'd steel himself against her leaving, and keep her at a distance...but he could still help her.

Willow and the baby were temporary. They were never going to be his responsibility long-term. So this was fine.

That was what he'd told himself over and over in the dark. What he'd repeated in his mind on the drive to the hospital. The thought that had kept him going as he'd gritted his teeth and followed those damn signs to the right department, and sat waiting.

But now, as he watched the image on the screen start to form and Willow squeezed his hand tightly, he wondered who he thought he was kidding.

He wasn't here because he thought it was safe. He was there because he couldn't imagine being anywhere else.

This is dangerous. This is the worst idea since your last terrible one, Gwyn. You need to get out, before this goes bad.

But he didn't. He ignored the sensible voice in his head and leaned closer, peering at the fuzzy picture on the screen.

'Here we go,' the technician said. 'Can you see the head, here?' She pointed to a white mass somewhere around the middle of the screen. 'Then this is the spine, down to the legs.'

In truth, it wasn't exactly a clear picture. Nothing you could really identify as an actual child.

But Willow's fingers squeezed his again, and his heart knew that was her baby on the screen, and that if he hadn't been here with her, if he'd left her to experience this alone, he would have always regretted it.

The technician checked everything looked okay, and confirmed the dating and due date.

'You're around seventeen weeks now, by the look of things,' she said. 'A little late for this scan, but it does mean we might even be able to see the sex, if you want?'

Willow nodded, then glanced up at him. 'I think so.'

He smiled, and shrugged—it wasn't his decision in the slightest. That said... 'I think any certainty you can add to this situation can only help.'

Willow's response was a watery chuckle, and the technician stayed professional enough not to respond at all, except to say, 'Okay then, let's take a look...'

CHAPTER EIGHT

TWENTY MINUTES LATER, they were back in the car park. Gwyn had given Willow the keys and told her to wait in the car while he sorted out paying for parking. She probably should have given him her credit card to pay, but she was too busy staring at the blurry, black and white printout the technician had given her to even think of it.

The driver's side door opened and Gwyn slipped in, closing it softly behind him. 'You okay?'

She nodded and said, 'Fine,' without considering whether it was true. It was just what you said when people asked, wasn't it?

Gwyn reached out and took the photo from her hand, holding it up between them so she automatically looked up at him. 'Let's try that again. You okay?'

This time, she took a moment, and a breath,

before answering. 'Honestly? I'm a little over-whelmed.'

'Understandable.' Gwyn turned the scan photo to study it himself. 'I mean, that's an actual person in there. That's pretty overwhelming.'

'Yeah.' Although, really, the living being *inside* her wasn't the problem.

It was what was going to happen when it was time for them to come out.

'I'm sorry they couldn't tell you if it was a boy or a girl,' Gwyn said.

Willow shrugged. 'At least she confirmed there's only one of them.' One baby was more than enough to be fretting about. Twins...that would have been a whole different level.

'You were worried it might be twins?'

'They do run in the family,' Willow pointed out.

'True.' Gwyn gave her back the photo and fastened his seatbelt before starting the engine. His shirtsleeves were rolled up—it had been warm in the hospital—and Willow found herself mesmerised by his bare forearms as he shifted the car into reverse, put one hand on the back of her seat and smoothly manoeuvred them out of the tight parking space.

She'd be lying if she denied that one of the

reasons she'd been glad Gwyn had agreed to take her to her appointment was that it gave her another opportunity to watch him drive. It was surprisingly sexy watching someone as attractive as Gwyn do anything well, and he really was a very good driver.

Of course, she'd also be lying if she pretended that was the *only* reason she'd been glad to have him there.

Willow wasn't afraid of doing this alone. In lots of ways, she'd been on her own since Rowan had left six years ago, and she'd been doing fine.

Okay, maybe not fine.

Her professional life had flourished, and she'd gone on to bigger and better campaigns, being recognised in the street and making more money than she could have dreamed of. She'd managed to put boundaries around her relationship with her mother, wrestling control of her own future from her in return for a *very* generous monthly stipend that Willow could now easily afford, and which kept her mother safely out of her business on the other side of the country.

She'd bought her Manhattan penthouse. She'd featured in magazines, on billboards, on runways, all over the world. She had the fame, money and career she'd always dreamed of. And most of that had happened since Rowan had left and she had to face the world alone.

But now, staring at that black and white image as the English countryside rushed past the windows, she wondered if she'd lost something else.

Someone to enjoy it all with, perhaps.

Oh, she had friends, and colleagues and acquaintances—she was close to her assistant, or had been, until she'd had to quit to look after her sick father, just before Willow had peed on that first stick. At the time, she'd thought that was a blessing—hiding the pregnancy symptoms from her would have been impossible. Now, she realised she'd lost one of the few pillars of personal support she had.

And she'd *paid* her to be in her life.

There was Ben, but he just didn't count, no matter how she looked at it. He was business as much as pleasure and, the last year or so, even the pleasure had been fleeting. He called when he needed her to appear with him, and she called when she had an itch to scratch because, honestly, they *were* in a relationship, however misguided, and she'd never been one for anonymous sex.

Finding anyone else was hard, anyway. Her

fame made her a target for people who wanted to use her, and she couldn't get away with pro-miscuity the way Ben could, just by virtue of being a man. At least Ben was upfront about what he was using her for. That had always seemed the lesser of two evils.

There was her mother, but...just no.

And there was Rowan. Her twin sister. The one person she knew would support her through anything. So she'd run to her and... instantly sent her away.

She knew all the reasons she'd done it, of course—had spent hours running through them in her head even before she'd landed in the UK. And she still believed it was probably the best solution to all their problems.

But it did leave her on her own again.

Alone. Except for Gwyn.

Gwyn, who clearly didn't want to get in-volved in all this but had anyway because he obviously saw how much she needed some-one, anyone.

How much of her growing feelings for him—the ones she was still trying desperately to pre-tend she didn't have, but failing more often than she succeeded—were just down to him being the only person in her corner when she needed him?

Maybe she was just feeling gratitude, and her hormones had confused it into lust.

That would explain a lot.

Gwyn pulled the car to a smooth stop outside her cottage and she jumped anyway, surprised they'd made it home so fast.

'You okay?' Gwyn asked again, his brow furrowed with concern as she fumbled to unfasten her seatbelt.

'Yeah. Just tired.' That was more convincing than fine, wasn't it?

From Gwyn's nod, it was. 'It's been a long day. Come on, let's get you inside.'

On another day, she might have asked him to stay for a cup of tea, or something. Today, she needed to be alone. She said her thankyous, took her bag and shut the door in his face—ignoring his obvious confusion as she did so.

She needed to think.

After an afternoon spent sitting at Rowan's kitchen table, thinking, Willow took a long, warm bath and went to bed for an early night. But sleep was a long time coming.

In fact, sleep continued to be elusive for the next few days, until the night she finally crashed out into a peaceful oblivion—only to be woken at the crack of dawn by her ringing phone.

She glanced blearily at the screen in the half light, and pressed answer. 'Rowan? What's the matter?'

Rowan's answer was a stream of words without pause, most of which didn't make any sense until Willow's tired brain managed to pick through them and choose only the ones that really mattered.

Eli. Truth. Ben. Needed to tell him.

Oh, this didn't sound good.

'Wait a minute,' she said, once Rowan was done. 'Are you sleeping with Ben's brother?' That was the only Eli Willow knew and, frankly, this sounded like a disastrous idea.

'No! We're just friends,' Rowan insisted. Willow was sure that while that might be *technically* true, it wasn't all either of them wanted.

Like me and Gwyn, maybe? No. Focus.

Rowan was still talking. 'I couldn't do anything more when I was still lying to him about something as basic as my actual name.'

'But you wanted to, right?' Willow guessed, trying not to project her feelings about Gwyn onto her sister and Eli. 'That's why you felt you had to tell him the truth. I can get that.' She sighed. At least she hadn't had to lie to

Gwyn, because he'd known the truth from the start. But she was still lying to his family, and everyone else in Rumbelow.

Maybe this hadn't been such a good idea, after all.

'Is everything okay? With the baby? The cottage?' Rowan asked. 'Ben hasn't been in touch, has he? Because honestly, the more I hear about that guy, the more I think you had the right idea, hiding out in Rumbelow.' At least one of them did.

'Even if it meant you had to make "friends" under false pretences?' Teasing was lots easier than dealing with this right now.

'Even then,' Rowan promised. 'Seriously, Will. Is everything okay?'

'Everything's fine,' Willow replied, hoping she sounded convincing. 'There's just…stuff. But I had my scan and we got to hear the baby's heartbeat and see it wriggling about and everything! Not enough for us to tell if it's a boy or a girl though. It had its legs crossed.'

'I want photos!' Rowan paused, and Willow could almost hear her frowning. 'Wait. We?'

Ah. Rookie error there. 'Me and the ultrasound technician.'

Rowan's pause was suspicious. 'Right. Well, send me photos.'

'I will,' Willow promised, pleased to have dodged that bullet. 'If *you* talk to Eli. Tell him whatever you need to, just make sure he doesn't tell Ben where I am or what's going on.'

She already knew what her sister was going to say before she said it.

'I'm going to tell him the truth, Will,' Rowan replied.

The tables had been turned, and Gwyn really didn't like it.

Yes, he'd been avoiding Willow, a bit. But now she was avoiding him and, well, that wasn't on. Not when he'd finally decided that it was okay to let her in, just a little, just for a while.

It wasn't that he was attracted to her. Okay, that was a lie. It wasn't *just* that he was attracted to her. Because of course she was one of the most beautiful women in the world, that was sort of a given for a straight guy, right?

But more than that, he *liked* her. He liked spending time with her. Liked the way she raised those perfectly arched eyebrows and asked him questions that got him talking about things he thought he'd packed away years ago, somewhere deep in his psyche. Not that he *wanted* to talk about them. But it just felt…

good for someone else to know everything that had happened, and why he was the way he was now.

Someone other than his sister, who could only ever look at him with excruciating pity when the subject came up.

Willow didn't pity him. She showed compassion and understanding, but not pity—maybe because she hadn't been there to witness firsthand how comprehensively he'd fallen apart.

Whatever it was, he wanted more of it. He knew it couldn't be more than friendship—she'd be leaving soon, and she was pregnant with another man's child, and that wasn't a mess he really wanted to be stuck in the middle of. No matter how tempting it might be—and no matter how certain he was he'd be better for her than the *actual* father of her child.

That wasn't the point. He wasn't looking for anything romantic—with anyone. Certainly not with someone who was starting a family and needed a reliable father figure to lean on.

Gwyn already knew he wasn't that man.

But friendship—short-term, without commitment or expectation, just helping a woman out because she deserved it rather than because she needed it, or him—that he could do.

Would do, even, if she wasn't avoiding him.

Which brought him back to his original problem.

Tonight was folk night again at the Star and Dragon, and he *knew* Willow had enjoyed it more than she'd expected when she'd joined him last time. If anything was going to tempt her out of isolation, it would be good music and excellent lasagne.

So he put his guitar in its case and headed down the hill to knock on her cottage door.

'Folk night? Again?' Willow looked confused at the idea when she answered.

'It's a weekly affair,' Gwyn said. 'And it's been a week. A few, actually.' Between him avoiding her and her avoiding him, they'd missed some.

'I realise that. I just... Aren't you worried? About showing up there with me twice, I mean?'

'Worried about what, exactly?' He suspected he knew, but he wanted to hear her say it. If only because hearing it out loud would probably remind her how silly it was.

'Worried that people will think we're, you know. Together. And then when I leave, or when news gets out about the baby...'

Gwyn raised his eyebrows. 'Since when

have you—or I, for that matter—cared what people around here think?'

Willow shook her head. 'I don't want to run back to New York and leave you here to deal with the gossip.'

Something about the way she said it gave him pause. 'Are you planning on going back soon?'

Wouldn't it be typical that, just when he'd decided to let her into his life, she'd decided to leave it?

But Willow shook her head, blonde hair shaking in front of her face. 'No. Not yet. At least, I hope not. I…' She looked up and smiled. 'Let me grab my coat and I'll tell you about it on the way to the pub.'

'Okay.' Gwyn grinned at her retreating back as she headed for the coat closet under the stairs, then caught himself and schooled his expression. It never did to be *too* enthusiastic about things.

'So, Rowan is confessing all over there in the States?' Gwyn summarised, after she'd re-counted her recent phone call with her sister.

'Looks like,' Willow said glumly. 'To Eli, anyway. Once she can persuade him to listen to her.'

'And is he likely to tell his brother?' Because from what Willow had now told him about her ex, once Ben found out that she was pregnant and hiding out in Cornwall, Gwyn couldn't believe they wouldn't see his private plane landing nearby very soon.

'I don't know.' Frustration leaked out of Willow's voice. 'I just don't know him well enough to tell.'

So she was in limbo, waiting to see if the axe was going to fall. Gwyn knew how that felt, and it was never fun. The best he could do was try to distract her this evening.

'Come on.' He looped her arm through his as they continued down the hill. 'I'll buy you a lime and soda and a lasagne to take your mind off it.'

'With garlic bread?' she asked hopefully.

Gwyn smiled. 'Definitely with garlic bread.'

As far as he was concerned, the evening was going entirely to plan. Thirty minutes later they were ensconced at what he'd already begun to think of as *their* table in the back, enjoying the music, the ambience and the lasagne. Sean and Kayla were up on stage again, and he was already running through his own possible set in his mind. He even had a new song he'd been working on he thought might be ready to debut. He wanted to hear what Willow thought of it.

'Another?' He raised his empty pint glass and nodded at Willow's similarly finished lime and soda. She nodded, her mouth full of lasagne, and so he headed to the bar.

Which was where his carefully constructed fantasy about the evening fell apart.

It took him a half a second to realise why the woman at the bar looked familiar. A moment longer to realise that she'd seen him too, and that the man at her side must be her husband. The man she'd left him for.

'Rachel.' He forced a polite smile. 'It's good to see you.'

A lie. It wasn't good. It tore at his insides still and to this day. Not because he still loved her, but because seeing her reminded him of all the reasons he'd never moved on. Why he and Willow could only ever be friends.

'And you.' Her smile looked fake too, but that might be because her husband was looking between the two of them in a way that suggested he was jumping to conclusions.

Gwyn held out a hand. 'I'm Gwyn. I used to know Rachel a long time ago.'

'Mark.' Rachel's husband shook his hand.

'And yes, I've heard of you. Are you playing tonight, then?'

'Oh, probably not.' He hoped they didn't look behind him to where his guitar was propped up beside Willow. Any intention he had of playing had now left the building.

'You're not playing?' Kayla and Sean had finished their first set and joined him at the bar, Kayla looking disappointed as she spoke. 'I thought Sean said you had a new song.'

'It's not ready yet,' Gwyn lied.

'That's a shame,' another voice said, and he felt his eyes close with the effort of not wincing. 'I was looking forward to hearing it. Hi, I'm Rowan.'

When he opened his eyes again, Willow was shaking hands with Rachel and Mark in turn, as if this was a perfectly normal situation.

As if his whole heart and history weren't sitting on the bar, about to be pounded with a mallet.

He knew that Willow had made the connection between his past and the woman in front of her the moment Mark made introductions. He felt her whole body press against his side, and she reached for his hand. To the other side he saw Kayla nudge Sean and look pointedly at their joined hands.

Oh, this whole night was getting out of control now.

'We've got a table over there, if you'd like to join us?' Willow said, and Gwyn's heart stopped just for a moment.

'Oh, no. Thank you, though,' Rachel said. 'We're here with friends.'

She pointed across the bar to a table of four people Gwyn vaguely recognised, all watching the drama unfolding at the bar with intense interest, until he looked over and they all quickly glanced away.

It was a very British drama, Gwyn supposed. One only really noticeable by the heaviness of the tension all around them. But people knew him. They knew Rowan. And enough of them knew Rachel to understand why he just wanted to drink himself under the bar right now, or at least get the hell out of there.

But he wouldn't. Because he had to make sure Willow got home safely.

Just another reason he shouldn't have let himself feel responsible for her, he supposed.

'I knew they'd say no,' Willow whispered as they made their way back to their table a moment later, after some more awkward goodbyes. 'I'd seen them greeting friends over there on their way in. Of course, I didn't know who she was then...'

Five minutes earlier, she'd been watching Gwyn at the bar, admiring the line of his body as he leant on his elbows, waiting for her drink. Then she'd seen the attractive brunette approach and greet him, the man at her side looking far less happy about the situation. She'd speculated, of course—old friend, fan of his music, family friend...

She'd only figured it out when Abigail had stopped by the table, spotted Gwyn at the bar, and cursed—then sent Sean and Kayla over there as some sort of buffer.

'I daren't go over there myself. I honestly don't know what I might do.' Abigail had dropped into Gwyn's empty chair. 'I can't believe she'd have the nerve to come here again, after everything she did.'

'That's Rachel, then?' Willow had guessed.

Abigail had looked surprised. 'He told you about her? Well, good. Hopefully, that means he's moving on at last. But yes, that's her.'

After that, it had been inevitable that Willow would go up and give Gwyn some moral support. What else was a friend supposed to do?

'You realise she thinks we're here together,'

Gwyn muttered under his breath as they reached their table. Abigail, thankfully, had gone, and they were alone—or as alone as they could be in a busy pub.

'Is that a problem?' Willow arched her eyebrows. 'I wouldn't have thought you'd be too worried who your *married* ex-girlfriend thinks you're dating.'

He flashed her an irritated look. 'I would have thought you *did* care who everyone in this village thinks *you're* dating. You know what gossip is like around here.'

Willow didn't point out that she'd only been there a couple of weeks so how could she know, because she *did* know. Even if Rowan believed that she lived in a bubble of privacy here, Willow knew that wasn't the case.

People *always* talked. And after tonight they'd be talking about *them*.

Not that she was about to admit to making a mistake or anything, though.

'I just thought I'd better get over there and support you before you started sobbing into the bar,' she said grumpily. 'I mean, that was the woman who broke your heart so badly you never recovered, wasn't it?'

Gwyn gave her an incredulous look. '*That's* what you got from that story?'

'It's what I got from your sister's swearing and concern the moment she saw her near you,' Willow replied.

He groaned. 'I take it that Abigail sent Sean and Kayla over, then?'

'She did.' Willow risked a small smile. 'I came on my own initiative.'

'Of course you did.' This time, when he looked across the table at her, the irritation in his expression had gone, replaced with a sort of exasperated fondness, if she was reading him right.

'I just didn't want to leave you alone with her,' she said softly.

'Thank you.' He reached across the table and squeezed her hand. 'I appreciate the show of support. But...' He looked up and glanced around the pub. Willow followed suit and quickly took his point.

Everywhere she turned, someone was just looking away from them, not wanting to be caught staring.

'Everyone in this pub thinks we're together now,' she finished for him.

She wasn't quite sure how she felt about that. On the one hand, she was already faking her whole existence—what was one more element of it?

On the other…if people were going to believe she was sleeping with Gwyn, it seemed incredibly unfair that she wasn't actually going to get to experience it.

She stamped that thought down.

'I'm sorry,' she said. 'I really did just want to support you. You looked…' Broken, she finished in her head. He'd looked broken. And just for a moment, she'd wondered if she *could* be the right person to put him back together again, after all. 'But I get that you don't want everyone in your home village thinking you're dating Rowan. Or even me, for that matter.'

Gwyn huffed a laugh. 'Are you kidding me? Do you really think there's a straight man on earth who wouldn't be just a little bit smug if people thought he was dating one of the Harper twins, even if it wasn't true?'

Willow looked away. Was that how Ben saw her? she wondered. She had a horrible feeling that it was. That Gwyn had just articulated *exactly* why the father of her child was with her in the first place.

Was she any better, though? She wasn't in love with Ben, so it had to be something else keeping her with him. Convenience, if nothing else.

God, how had she got herself into this mess?

Cool fingers touched her chin, bringing her gaze back to Gwyn's. 'That's not why I'm here with you. You know that, right?'

'Why are you?' she asked, feeling strangely vulnerable as he held both her face and her gaze.

He hesitated for a second, and she instantly regretted asking it. That was the question she should be asking Ben—why he was with her, at least until they'd broken up, and was there a chance of a happy future for them?

'I'm here with you because I don't seem able to stay away,' he admitted.

Willow stared at him, then looked away to gather her thoughts before she replied. Because the truth was she couldn't stay away from him either—if she could, she'd have said no when he'd shown up to invite her to the Star and Dragon that night. She'd have left him alone at the bar with his ex and her husband. She wouldn't have invited him to the baby scan in the first place.

Gwyn dropped his hand from her face as she moved, and she reached out across the table to grab it, squeezing his fingers between her own, trying to convey that she wasn't pulling away—just pulling herself together.

'I got another message from Rowan while

you were at the bar, telling me not to look on-
line for Ben,' she said. Her sister had also in-
formed her that she'd told Ben's brother Eli
the truth about who she was and why she was
there, but that Eli had promised to keep their
secret—for now.

'So you instantly looked him up?' Gwyn
guessed.

'Of course,' she replied. 'He's out on some
superyacht with a woman probably fifteen
years his junior, proving he doesn't need me.'

'I'm sorry. That's got to hurt.' Despite everything, Gwyn did sound genuinely sorry.

'It doesn't,' Willow admitted. 'It doesn't hurt
at all. Which, if I needed further evidence that
we're not meant to be together, would probably do it.' She sighed. 'It doesn't make anything much easier though because…the man's
practically a child himself. He's doing this for
the people watching—the media, the cameras,
the gossip sites. The exact same reason he was
dating me. And…that's not the life I want for
my child.'

'Are you reconsidering whether you tell him
about the baby at all?' There was no judgement
in Gwyn's voice, even though she knew he had
to have serious feelings about it, given his past.

'No,' she reassured him. 'Even if I wanted

to—which I don't—his brother knows now, and he's not going to keep that secret for ever. It wouldn't be fair to ask him to either.'

'So…what's changed?' Gwyn asked. 'You said when you told me about the baby in the first place that you didn't think you should raise it with Ben. What's different now?'

It was a good question, one she weighed up in her head for a moment or two before she answered. 'Certainty, I suppose.' She sighed. 'Maybe there was a part of me hoping that this time he'd grow up, learn a lesson, realise that he wanted me more than he wanted whatever he's out there getting right now. And I'd realise that I did love him after all, and we could all live happily ever after.'

'But that didn't happen,' Gwyn finished for her.

She gave him a soft smile. He didn't even realise how much of this was because of him.

'No, it didn't,' she said. '*You* happened instead.'

CHAPTER NINE

'ME?' GWYN BLINKED, unsure what to make of this sudden conversational U-turn.

They'd been talking about everyone thinking they were together, then about Ben, and now... he wasn't sure. He'd only had two pints, but that was enough to render Willow's conversational meanderings indecipherable.

But he knew it was important. Whatever she was trying to say...it mattered. And he was going to listen carefully until he got it.

'I don't... What do *I* have to do with it?' He wasn't going to make any assumptions either. That was definitely a sure-fire way to get them both into trouble.

Her smile was gentle. With her blonde hair falling around her shoulders, and the way she leaned across the table towards him, he couldn't blame everyone around them for thinking they were on a date.

He wasn't one hundred per cent sure himself, right now.

'You found me a midwife and made me an appointment and took me there. You drove me to my scan and held my hand when I was nervous. You hugged me when I was over-whelmed. You shared your past with me, even when it was hard. You brought me here to help me get to know the village. You even let me join your family for Sunday dinner, and get to know your sister and nephew.' She was still smiling, so he figured that was a good thing. And when she laid it out like that...maybe he had let her into his life rather a lot more than he'd realised.

'Do you know,' she went on, 'I've never even met Ben's brother, Eli? Rowan seems to have met him her first day in New York, but Ben never, ever introduced us. He never let me into any part of his life that wasn't for show. I don't think I even fully realised it until I came here and things with you were so...different.'

Did that mean she was getting ideas? Think-ing he was going to step into Ben's shoes and help her raise this kid? Because the only rea-son he'd let himself get as close as he had was because he knew she was leaving soon.

Even if the idea of her going, of never seeing the baby born or seeing Willow be a mother, had started to cause a steady ache in the centre of his chest.

'Willow, I—'

She held up a hand to stop him. 'I'm not asking you for anything here, Gwyn. Don't worry. I know you're not interested in me that way—I mean, why would you be? I'm pregnant and hormonal and, if these jeans are any indication because they're *already* only held together by a hairband around the button, I'm going to get huge over the next few months. And I'm leaving soon, we both know that.'

He nodded, trying very hard to concentrate on her words and not the picture in his head of her, round with baby and smiling at him, one hand on her bump, the other reaching for him...

'I'm just saying that you, as a friend, showed me what I should expect from a partner. And I know for sure now that Ben doesn't have it in him.'

'Good.' The word came out as a fierce sort of half growl that surprised even Gwyn. But the idea of Willow going back to Ben after this set something on fire inside him, even if he wasn't willing to name the feeling just yet. 'He doesn't deserve you.'

Neither did he, of course, but that was beside the point. Willow didn't *need* any man at her side anyway. If she chose to have someone there...that person should just be grateful to be chosen.

'I think we both deserve more,' Willow said, which was more diplomatic than Gwyn would have managed, but also very true. 'We don't love each other. And I think... I think I have to give all my love to my kid now, anyway. For now, at least. Because if it's only going to have one parent, I need to be the best mum I can possibly be, right? Better than my own, at least.'

'Sounds like you've made your mind up what to do, then.' Gwyn took a sip of his pint to hide how uncertain he felt about that. If she'd decided her path she'd be leaving soon, and he was willing to at least admit to himself that he'd miss her company. But already he cared about her enough to want her to go, if that was the right thing for her.

She gave him a lopsided smile. 'I still need to figure out exactly what I want that to look like, but being here, clearing my head...it's helped a lot in enabling me to picture it.'

'That's good.' And it was good. He just had to keep telling himself that—and ignore the pain in his chest that just kept increasing. 'I guess you'll be heading home to New York soon, and I'll get my old, less outgoing neighbour back. And I mean "outgoing" literally, of course, since Rowan hates going out anywhere.'

That made her laugh, which was his intention, but her expression turned quickly pensive as she studied him across the table. 'Soon, I suppose. But not just yet. I'm not quite done with Rumbelow and all it has to offer yet.'

Gwyn couldn't put his finger on what exactly had changed, but with her words the whole night felt different. Sean and Kayla were back on stage, striking up a new song, one with a low and sensuous melody. The air seemed to buzz, thick with…something. Anticipation? Heat?

It was definitely heat. He could feel it in Willow's gaze, not to mention inside his own body. Filling him up from his belly outwards. Or maybe slightly lower than his belly, if he was honest.

He tightened his fingers around his pint glass. 'You have plans for the rest of your stay?'

There was a vulnerability behind her gaze now too. One that made him want to reassure her. 'Well, that depends a lot on you.'

Couldn't she tell? Didn't she know she'd

held him in her thrall almost since the moment she'd arrived in the village?

His mind flashed back to her earlier words and he realised—she didn't. The woman voted most beautiful in the world more than once wasn't sure if he desired her. Even as he was sitting here aching with wanting her.

He placed his pint down on the table and reached for her hand, tracing patterns on the back of it as he stared into her eyes.

'You said something before, and I should have corrected you at the time,' he said, low and serious. 'You said...you said you knew I couldn't be interested in you, all pregnant and hormonal. And you were right in a way—I'm not looking for any kind of relationship, you know that. But the idea that I'm not attracted to you... Willow, pregnant or not, you're the most beautiful woman I've ever seen in real life. But that's not why I want you so damn badly.'

Her breath hitched and he watched her eyes widen even further. 'Why, then?'

'Because you're *you*. Because you're trying so damn hard to do the right thing by your baby, whatever that turns out to be. Because you *listen*—not just to my sob stories, but to everyone. Because you give off the kind of

energy that is just irresistible. And because...
when I'm near you every inch of my body
aches to touch every inch of yours.'

She held his gaze for a long, long moment.
Then she pushed away her still half full glass
and got to her feet.

'Let's get out of here,' she said.

Gwyn downed the rest of his pint and followed.

Outside, the night was dark and a chill was
blowing in from the sea, cold enough to make
Willow pause and wonder what the hell she
was doing, dragging Gwyn up the hill behind
her towards her cottage.

Not cold enough to make her stop, though.

They'd got as far as the street outside the pub
when he realised he'd forgotten his guitar and
had to go back for it. She was taking that as a
good sign—a sign that he was as blindsided by
this as she was. She could *feel* the want and the
need pulsing in her veins in a way she never
had before. Certainly not with Ben.

Not thinking about him tonight.

In fact, thinking altogether was off the agenda
for tonight. Tonight, she just wanted to feel. To
be herself, rather than a mother-to-be. To forget every reason she had not to be doing this.

One last selfish indulgence, before her whole life changed and she had to adjust and adapt to always putting someone else first.

They didn't speak until they were outside the gate to her cottage, all energy going into just getting there—fast. Willow was breathing hard as she swung the gate open, only to find Gwyn hovering outside the edge of the cottage boundary.

'Are you sure about this?' he asked.

She liked that he didn't pretend to not know what they were there for, or to hedge his bets in case he got shot down at the last moment. She liked that he asked too.

'I'm leaving soon,' she said bluntly. 'And you don't want anything more than short-term fun anyway, right?' He nodded. 'So let's make the most of the time I have left here. Before everything changes.'

He didn't hesitate again.

Inside, the cottage felt smaller with two of them in it. Maybe they should have gone to his spacious home, but it was further away and, really, who could spare the time?

He dropped his guitar case by the front door, and she'd stripped his jacket from his shoulders before it hit the floor.

She surged up before she could change her

mind, her mouth meeting his as he wrapped strong arms around her waist, hauling her closer. The heat that had been building between them all evening—longer, since the hug in the doctor's car park, since the day they'd met—exploded into a supernova. Every inch of her skin vibrated with the feel of him. His hand in her hair, the other at the small of her back, keeping her close. The hard ridge that pressed against her belly. His lips, moving across her jaw, down her throat to her collarbone and making her shiver.

'Bedroom,' she whispered, close to his ear, and he nodded.

They stumbled there together, shedding clothes between them as they went, leaving a trail from the front door to the bed. For once, Willow didn't care about the mess.

She fell backwards onto the bed with barely a jolt and he was right there above her, on top of her, his hands then his mouth at her breasts, then working their way down her body, over her slightly rounded stomach, until he knelt between her parted thighs, his mouth making her writhe and scream as the world seemed to contract then expand to contain so much more than it had before.

'Okay?' Gwyn murmured, and when had he got back up here, lying beside her on the bed?

She reached out and pulled him closer again. 'More than.'

'Good. In that case…' He hauled her up until she sat astride him, and the desperate want of him started to curl in her belly again.

'Do we need anything?' She was already pregnant, and she knew she was clean—had been tested the moment she knew she was pregnant, just in case.

'I haven't been with anyone since my last tests,' he told her, and she trusted him. More than anyone else right now.

'Me neither.'

She lifted her thighs, reaching under her to position him, before sinking down onto him, her eyes closing with the sensation of being so filled, so complete.

God, she'd needed this.

Beneath her, Gwyn moaned, his hands grabbing her hips to steady her as she started to move, picking up the pace with every flick of her hips, until the friction between them, the rise and the fall, the push and the pull, threatened to drive her mad.

When she lost the rhythm, consumed with sensation, he held on tight and moved her for them, thrusting up into her until she fisted her hands in the sheets beneath them, threw back her head and moaned so loud the fish in the sea must have heard it. At the sound, she felt Gwyn tense beneath her too, and curse softly, before lowering her down to rest her head against his shoulder.

'We really should have done that before now,' she murmured.

He chuckled, the sound vibrating through her. 'Trust me. We're definitely going to be doing it again soon. To make up for lost time.'

The morning sun streamed through an unfamiliar window, and Gwyn blinked at the light, shifting against the sheets—until he realised he wasn't alone, and the events of the past evening took shape in his memory.

He smiled.

A proper, purely happy and satisfied smile.

When was the last time he'd smiled one of those? He couldn't remember.

He pressed a kiss to the top of the blonde head that rested on his shoulder, and contemplated waking her up. But Willow looked so peaceful, sleeping in his arms, that he couldn't bring himself to.

Instead, he checked in with himself, searching for regret, anxiety, any of the usual feelings he'd have around now if he'd let himself get a fraction as close to someone as he'd grown close to Willow.

It wasn't there.

It was because he knew she was leaving, he decided. This couldn't last, because she'd be going home to New York soon. That made it safe. That meant he could enjoy it while it lasted—then go back to his usual existence.

Oh. There was that black cloud. Damn. And it had been going so well.

Willow stirred beside him, making a frankly adorable little noise as she woke. She blinked up at him and smiled, bright and sunny, for a moment. Then she bit down on her lip.

'Do we need to talk about this?' she asked, her voice husky with sleep.

Gwyn shook his head. 'Let's just enjoy it while we can,' he replied, and kissed her down into the mattress again.

Eventually, though, they had to get out of bed. Gwyn made them breakfast, pottering around Rowan's kitchen in a way that felt both right and weird at the same time. He glanced back at Willow, sitting at the kitchen table with a cup of decaf coffee between her hands. That part felt right.

It was the strange disconnect, he supposed, of being in Rowan's space with a woman who *looked* like Rowan but wasn't. Not at all. He'd never felt about Rowan the way he felt about Willow.

Not that he intended to examine those feelings too closely. What was the point, when he knew she'd be leaving soon and it would all be moot anyway? No, the built-in expiry date was the only reason this was possible, so he wasn't going to fret about it. At all.

At least, not intentionally.

He'd had a moment, somewhere in the middle of their second time round last night, where he'd belatedly worried about the baby, then remembered the pamphlets he'd read at the hospital that told him sex was perfectly safe for most pregnant women. He hadn't realised he'd tucked away that piece of information at the time, but he was glad now that he had.

Willow was still barely showing at the moment, but from what little he knew of pregnancy—mostly gleaned from those hospital pamphlets, rather than paying attention to his sister's own pregnancy, since he'd been considerably less interested in that side of the female body's workings back then—it wouldn't be long before she really started to round out.

He wondered if she'd still be in Rumbelow then. If he'd get to feel the weight of her belly as it grew. See her round and glowing with her child.

Her child.

Would she come back and visit, Rowan at least, after the baby was born? Or would she expect her twin to fly out to New York to visit her, now she'd persuaded her to do it once?

Would he ever get to meet the baby Willow was carrying?

It seemed more of a possibility now she'd made a firm and final choice to raise the child alone, rather than with Ben. But still not guaranteed. He wasn't sure how he felt about never meeting the baby whose growth and wellbeing he'd been so closely involved with the last few weeks.

'Gwyn? I think the toast is burning…' Willow was suddenly beside him, reaching for the grill, until he stopped her and used the oven gloves to open it without burning either of them.

'Sorry. Lost in thought.'

'Reliving last night?' Willow guessed with a satisfied grin.

'Something like that.' He couldn't tell her the truth—that he was afraid he might be missing her before she'd even gone.

She couldn't stay. And he couldn't let himself feel the way about her that he did if she *was* staying.

He didn't have room in his life, or his broken heart and damaged psyche, to feel responsible for another person—two people, even, counting the baby. He knew himself, knew how little of the person he used to be was left after everything that had happened to those around him.

If Willow got hurt. If the *baby* was hurt—and children did get hurt, didn't they? They had accidents and broken bones and health scares. And they grew into teenagers and then young adults like Sean, and the capacity for tragedy and disaster was just all the greater.

It would break him for good if something happened to Willow and the baby on his watch. Or, at the same time, to Abigail or Sean while he was looking out for Willow.

He knew his limits, and he was at them. Pushing them already, if he was honest, just by getting involved with Willow at all.

If he let himself love her—

'Breakfast.' He turned away from the counter, sharply cutting off his thoughts, and placed

Willow's plate in front of her. She dug in with gusto and he watched with satisfaction.

'What did you want to do today?' she asked between mouthfuls. Then she caught herself and added, 'Not that I'm suggesting you have to stay and do things with me, that's not the deal. Certainly not beyond the bedroom door. But I don't have any plans, and—'

He decided to put her out of her misery. 'Today? Today I think we should spend here, preferably in bed. But tomorrow... Tomorrow is the village fete. The May fair, or whatever. We could go, if you like.'

'Together?' That was right. They hadn't talked about what this meant in public, had they.

'As friends,' he clarified.

'Friends who the whole village already think are sleeping together.' She gave him a wicked grin. 'Works for me.'

CHAPTER TEN

THE VILLAGE FETE was everything Willow imagined it should be. It had taken over every inch of Rumbelow, it seemed—from the playing field to the closed-off streets to the beach itself. There was bunting, a small carousel, homemade jam stalls, a local brass band playing and schoolchildren doing some sort of dance with ribbons in the village square. Down on the beach, there were short boat rides, freshly caught seafood to buy and a sandcastle competition.

It was perfect.

She tried to imagine what it must be like, growing up in this place as a child, and couldn't quite. It was probably lonely in the winter, right? When all the tourists had gone.

Except the town today was bustling with locals as well as visitors, and almost everyone nodded and said hi. It was hard to imagine ever being lonely in Rumbelow.

Her phone buzzed in her pocket and she ignored it. Again.

At her side, Gwyn glanced down at her pocket. He was walking close enough to her that he must have felt the vibration, but not actually holding her hand or touching her in any way in case people got the wrong—or right—idea. It felt strange not to be able to touch him, after being so intimate. But she understood. Soon, it would be Rowan here, and she didn't want the village assuming her sister was sleeping with Gwyn. No, she really, really didn't want that—even if she wasn't keen on delving into her subconscious right now to figure out why the idea made acid rise up her throat.

Probably that was just pregnancy heartburn anyway.

The phone buzzed again.

'Don't you need to answer that?' Gwyn asked mildly.

Willow shook her head. 'They're not for me. They're for Rowan.'

'How can you know that?' He frowned. 'And why are they messaging you anyway?'

With a sigh, Willow pulled out the phone to show him her notifications screen. Emails, direct messages, texts, voicemails…all technically for Willow, but not really. Not that he could really tell that about the voicemails, but the text preview on the others should make it obvious.

'They want you to design a dress?' His frown was even deeper and more confused now. 'But you don't— Oh!'

'Exactly. Rowan designed a dress for someone to wear to the gala dinner she went to the other week in New York, and once word got out who the designer was everybody wanted one. Except she's still pretending to be me, so...'

'So people think *you* designed the dress.'

'Yup.' Willow shoved her phone back into her pocket with a sigh. 'I'm forwarding them on to Rowan in batches, every hour or so.' And then *she* was ignoring them, as far as Willow could tell. Maybe they were more alike than she'd always thought.

'Come on.' She tucked her hand through Gwyn's arm. That didn't scream relationship, did it?—totally a friendly thing to do—and led him towards the stalls by the church that seemed to be selling some delicious-looking cakes. 'I want to take a look around.'

They pottered happily around the May Fair, taking in the sights, sounds and smells—and indulging in good coffee and better sweet treats. Gwyn didn't pull her arm away from his, and for a long moment or two it almost felt real.

As if they were really there together, a happy couple, expecting their first child, with a traditional happy ever after awaiting them.

Then a cloud would pass across the sun, making her shiver, or someone Gwyn knew would greet them and she'd feel him shrink away, and she knew none of it was true. She was an imposter, pregnant with another man's child, and none of this was her future.

Her future was thousands of miles away, in a city that never slept, alone.

Even she couldn't blame herself for fantasising for a day.

But when it came down to it, was it what she really wanted? Not Gwyn, specifically—although, really, she could have and had done a hell of a lot worse—but that idyllic, movie-perfect ending?

She pondered the question as she sat on the edge of the beach, perched on the stone wall that separated the steps from the sand, swinging her legs a little as she waited for Gwyn to return with ice cream, even though it was really still a little too cold for it at the very start of May.

It was the ending that every woman was conditioned to want, wasn't it? The handsome partner, the family, the big wedding—ideally not in that order, but that boat had sailed. The happy ending.

Except...what ended, then? The woman's single life, sure, but what about her hopes and dreams, her goals, her career, her future? Getting married didn't mean saying goodbye to those things, and neither did becoming a mother. Not any more.

Surely it was really just another sort of beginning? An exciting one, if she approached it right.

Besides, if she'd wanted that traditional happy ending she'd have told Ben straight off and married him—and been miserable. So that was already out of the window.

But that didn't mean there weren't elements of this accidental charade she'd fallen into with Gwyn that she *would* want in her future. The great sex for a start.

No, focus. This wasn't about that.

Okay, it wasn't *just* about that. She wasn't going to deny that it was an important part of things.

But so was the support. The companionship. Having someone there to hold her hand in the hospital. A wider circle of family and friends to belong to. Someone to queue for ice cream. Someone to support her—and for her to support in return. To listen to. To love.

Yes. She wanted all that. She knew for a fact that Gwyn couldn't give it to her longer term—he'd been very clear about his position on that. But, regardless, he had shown her what she wanted.

She'd always be grateful to him for that.

Willow folded her hands in her lap, beside the tiny bump of her stomach that was only going to keep growing from here, and looked to see where Gwyn had got to with the ice cream. She spotted him walking back across the sand towards her and raised a hand to wave, when something else caught her eye.

A phone, raised and pointed at her.

Taking a photo.

Gwyn caught sight of the guy in his early twenties with the phone from the corner of his eye and realised the man was approaching Willow only a second or so later.

Swearing under his breath, he picked up speed—as fast as he could over the soft, dry sand and without dropping their ice creams.

Willow was in broad daylight; she didn't need rescuing, but she might need backup.

'You're her, aren't you, though?' the guy was saying as Gwyn got closer. 'Willow Harper. I recognised you from the internet. My girl-friend said it couldn't be, but it is, isn't it?' He held up his phone proudly. 'This photo is going to get me so many hits!'

Willow shifted away a little further along the wall she was sitting on. 'I'm afraid you've made a mistake,' she said coldly. 'I'm *Rowan* Harper. Willow's my twin sister. I'm not a ce-lebrity, and I'd appreciate it if you respected my privacy.'

The guy's smile only broadened. 'That's even better! You're a *recluse*. You just disappeared! Hell, people might even pay me money for a photo of you!'

And that, Gwyn realised, was why Rowan had stayed in Rumbelow so long, and only gone to New York under duress and pretend-ing to be Willow. Here, she had the protection of the community. Yes, they all knew who she was, but they respected her privacy and nobody made a big deal about her past. She tended to avoid events like this, he remembered, a little too late, probably for this very reason.

'Here you go, sweetheart.' Gwyn pushed past

the guy with the phone and handed Willow her ice cream. 'But we'd better get going now, if we want to make…that thing in time.'

'Right, yes.' She hopped down from the wall and he steadied her elbow. Her centre of gravity was changing, he realised. That, or the sand and the confrontation with camera phone guy had her off-balance. Either way, he was taking her home.

He took her arm and led her away, neither of them speaking until they were well out of earshot of the intrusive tourist.

'Well, that was close,' Gwyn murmured.

Willow shook her head, glossy blonde hair brushing his shoulder. It made him think of the night before, of her hair hanging down over his chest as she moved above him…

Focus. There'd be time for that later.

'We knew it was only a matter of time,' she said, staring out towards the horizon. He didn't think she was seeing the trappings of a small coastal village's May fair, though.

If he had to guess, he'd say she was seeing New York.

No. Not yet. He wasn't ready.

She couldn't stay, he knew that. But he wasn't ready for her to go yet either. And he knew that was a problem, but…right in that moment, he couldn't bring himself to care.

'Let's go home,' he said urgently. 'I picked up some great decaf coffee from one of the stalls—let's go try it.'

'Yeah, okay.' She turned to him with a smile and, for now at least, he knew he'd won her back. Back to him and Rumbelow and forgetting about the future and everything else that was coming down the road.

And he intended to make the most of it while it lasted.

The coffee had been spectacular—even if it was decaf. Gwyn brewed it in the shiny silver stovetop coffee pot she'd sent Rowan for Christmas a few years ago and which had clearly never been used before.

'Now you'll have no reason at all to come all the way up to my house.' Gwyn laughed as she moaned at the first sip.

She eyed him warmly. 'I can think of a few reasons.'

Now, Willow stretched out against the sheets, thinking that they really should make the effort to get up to the lifeboat station, though. She quite fancied a night in Gwyn's bed. Still, she slept well in his arms wherever they were.

So well she'd slept in. Well, they'd woken up for breakfast in bed hours ago…but that had led to other things in bed, and now it was early afternoon. She supposed there was a chance they might make it as far as Gwyn's house tonight…and besides, after yesterday's encounter she was perfectly happy to hide away and wait for the bank holiday weekend tourists to leave.

Gwyn was still fast asleep beside her, so she carefully slipped out from between the sheets and reached for his T-shirt, pulling it over her head. It barely hit her thighs, so she pulled on her own underwear in the name of decency—and out of respect for any of the day-trippers out on the boats who could see straight through Rowan's kitchen windows. Then she headed out to find more of that coffee.

She found her phone first, though, because it was buzzing so hard it almost fell off the kitchen counter. More messages for Rowan, she assumed. She picked it up, intending to switch off the vibrate function for a while, when the notifications screen caught her eye and froze her heart.

Not messages for Rowan—not all of them, anyway.

There were eight voicemails from Ben.

Eight.

That wasn't a sensible, just catching up or checking in number.

That was a something has gone wrong number.

She needed to listen to them. To find out what was happening.

Steeling herself, she pressed play—then held the phone away from her ear.

After listening to the first one, she tried to call Rowan but got no answer. So she went back to listen to the others.

Certain phrases jumped out of each one.

'I know everything.'

'Thought you could hide?'

'Try to fool me?'

'Take me for an idiot?'

'I know, I know, I know...'

But mostly it was the rage, the fury in his voice that came through in each message. Her chest tightened as if it was collapsing in around a sudden rock buried there.

She pressed delete.

Before she could call Rowan again, the phone started to vibrate once more in her hand.

Not Ben this time, she realised with relief. Rowan. Thank God.

She swiped to answer the video call.

'Rowan? What's going on?' she asked before her sister could say anything at all. 'I've got, like, eight voicemails on my phone from Ben suddenly telling me he knows everything, and then you weren't answering yours and—'

'He doesn't know about the baby,' Rowan said quickly, her eyes wide on the screen. 'He does know I'm not you.'

'How?' Had Eli told him? No, Rowan had said he wouldn't. Had the photo from that guy's camera phone hit the internet even quicker than she'd thought? But he'd believed her when she'd said she was Rowan, she was sure. So who? And how?

Rowan explained the events of her morning and Willow tried not to laugh. She was perfectly happy to ignore the Ben part of this story and focus on her sister's misadventures—it was far more fun, for a start.

'Wait, so Eli was naked in bed with you when Ben walked in? Oh, my God!' This definitely sounded more like something Willow would do than Rowan. 'When did this happen? What's the deal with the two of you? Is this a drunken hook-up or something more…?'

'It's…not a drunken hook-up.' Rowan's

cheeks turned pink. No, of course it wasn't—
Rowan didn't do that sort of thing.

Willow grinned. She'd *known* sending her
twin to New York was a good idea.

'So it's something more.' Willow sat up a
little straighter at Rowan's kitchen table and
said, 'Tell me everything.'

Rowan opened her mouth, then closed it
again. And when she spoke, it wasn't the sala-
cious and sexy gossip Willow had been hoping
for. 'What's the point? I'm packing to come
home right now. So, whatever it was, I just
have to leave it here in New York.'

Willow's eyes widened. That was not where
she'd thought this was going. 'Okay. This is
clearly a conversation that needs tea. Go put
the kettle on and I'll do the same, and while it's
brewing you can tell me exactly what's been
going on over there between the two of you.'
She'd planned on coffee, but this conversation
really did call for tea, somehow. Maybe it was
just another way of feeling connected with her
sister, across an ocean.

Willow reached for the teapot from the top
shelf, tugging Gwyn's T-shirt down with the
other hand and hoping that her sister didn't notice she was wearing someone else's clothes.

Did she have time to go grab her jeans? Probably not without waking Gwyn up.

'I don't know where to begin,' Rowan admitted.

'Start from the beginning,' Willow advised. 'Right from the moment you arrived in New York and found him in my apartment. Because I'm pretty sure you've been leaving things out in your accounts of your Big Apple adventures, haven't you?' It made a change for her to be the one listening to *Rowan's* wild adventures. Usually, this was the other way around. But maybe she was going to have to get used to it. After all, she'd be a *mother* soon.

Rowan didn't deny it. Instead, she started talking—and once she'd started, it seemed like she couldn't stop.

'Well, it all sounds pretty much fairy tale perfect to me,' Willow said when she'd finished. 'Up until the part where my ex-boyfriend walked in. But he's *my* problem, not yours. So why aren't you happy? Why aren't you loved up and making dresses for celebrities and living your best life with Eli right now?' She should be. That was what she'd sent her to New York for.

Oh, fine. She hadn't *known* that this would happen when she'd asked Rowan to go. But she'd hoped that *something* would. Her sister deserved a little fun.

'Because…' Rowan took a breath and started again. 'When I came here, I was pretending to be you. So I lived life as if I *was* you, as best as I could. I took chances and put myself out there…all that stuff I haven't done since I walked out on you and Mum years ago. And I know… I know that was probably the idea—and don't think we're not going to have a conversation about why you decided sending me to New York was the best solution to your situation because we are, once I'm over this particular crisis.'

'I have no idea what you're talking about,' Willow said innocently. 'But go on.'

'These last few weeks…they haven't felt like real life. My real life is *there,* in Rumbelow. And the person I've been here… I can't be sure if she's real either. I miss my cottage, my home. And I miss the person I am there too, a little.'

Oh. Well, Willow knew that feeling. Being here in Rumbelow had been like a holiday for her too—an escape from reality. But she still knew she had to go back and face that reality, sooner rather than later.

But she had a feeling there was something

more going on for Rowan here. So she decided
to test the theory.

'So come home,' Willow said. 'Leave Eli
behind as a fond memory. A holiday fling.'

'I would. Except…'

'Except you're in love with him,' Willow
crowed triumphantly, almost upsetting her cup
of tea as she thumped the table with one hand.

Rowan's eyes went very wide, her face white
as chalk. Willow half expected her mouth to
start flapping like a fish.

But finally she said, 'Oh, God, I'm in love
with Eli.'

Of course she was. Willow could see that
from thousands of miles away. And now Rowan
could see it too. Everything was going to work
out! Maybe Rowan would even move to New
York and then she'd be around to be a part
of her niece or nephew's life, and everything
would be—

'I still can't stay here,' Rowan said, and Willow felt the daydream disappear.

'Why not?' she demanded. 'You love him,
you're glowing, he makes you happy, it's the
greatest city in the world, you've conquered
your fears of being out there again… You *can*
do this, Ro.'

'I… I feel like two people right now, Will.

The old Rumbelow Rowan and the new New York one,' Rowan said, obviously trying to explain a feeling she perhaps didn't fully understand herself yet. 'I need to find a way to make those two people one, before I can really move forward with my life.'

Well, Willow supposed she could empathise with that one. The person she was here in Rumbelow didn't feel much like the woman she'd been in New York either.

'And you need to come back to Rumbelow to do that?' she asked.

'I think so. Yes,' Rowan said, firmer this time.

'Then come home.' A small noise across the room made Willow glance up and see Gwyn standing in the doorway, arms folded across his broad, bare chest. She smiled at him, then turned back to her sister. 'You have to be sure, and you have to feel right about the decisions you're making. That's why *I* came here, after all. So come home and see if Rumbelow can work its magic on you.'

'Did it do that for you?' Rowan asked.

Willow didn't look back at Gwyn as she nodded. 'Yeah, I think it did. I'm ready to face the music now, anyway. This place has taught me what I want, and now all that's left is to make it happen.' Which meant leaving. Leaving Gwyn, specifically.

'That's good.'

'Perhaps Eli will come to Rumbelow with you,' Willow said hopefully.

Maybe Gwyn will visit New York some time.

'Perhaps,' Rowan echoed.

But she didn't sound very hopeful.

Willow knew how she felt.

CHAPTER ELEVEN

'YOU'RE LEAVING.'

He hadn't meant to say the words, they just tumbled out of him the moment Willow hung up on her call with Rowan. He bit down on the inside of his cheek to keep himself from saying more, and stayed where he stood in the doorway, even though every part of him was aching to go to her.

'Ben knows that Rowan isn't me.' She sounded tired—bone-weary—as she rubbed a hand across her forehead, tossing her phone down onto the table. 'It won't take him long to piece together where I am—especially if the guy from yesterday puts that photo up on social media.' She gave a wry smile. 'I should have let him keep believing I was Willow; one more photo of me wouldn't show up in a search. A new photo of Rowan will though. She's been AWOL for years.'

'You don't have to go running back to him,

you know.' Gwyn couldn't make sense of the swirl of feelings in his gut. Of course she was going to go home to the city where she lived. And of course she was going to want to speak to the father of her child. This had been the plan all along.

So why did it feel so wrong?

Willow looked up in surprise. 'I'm not *running back to him*. I'm just done hiding, that's all. It's time to face the music.' She took a deep breath and got to her feet. 'I'm ready.'

I'm not.

He wasn't ready to say goodbye to her. To let her walk out of his life. And suddenly…he wasn't sure he would ever be.

This was a disaster.

He'd only let himself get close to her *because* she was leaving. Because he knew he wouldn't have time to feel responsible for her—let alone the baby. To add that impossible weight to the one he already carried. To know that sooner or later he'd let her down and she'd get hurt, just like all the others.

He'd kept his distance—an emotional one, anyway, since the physical one had gone out of the window. But now, when it mattered, it didn't seem to make any difference.

He didn't want her to go.

'I should, uh, let you pack, then.'

'You don't have to—I probably won't be able to get a flight until at least tomorrow, anyway.'

They stood awkwardly with the kitchen table between them, the tension heavy. Was this goodbye? It should be. But she made him weak. And walking away…it felt impossible.

Until his phone rang.

He broke away from watching her and checked the screen instead—Abigail. He answered it without hesitation.

'Everything okay?'

He knew from her wrenching sob on the other end of the line that it wasn't. 'They've *gone,* Gwyn. Scott and Kayla. They…they left a note.'

'Gone where?' He knew the answer, though. Every tensed muscle in his body told him before she did.

'London. They said…they said that if we wouldn't support their dreams they'd just have to chase them alone. I *knew* I should have—'

'I'll be right there.' He hung up without listening to any more and turned to Willow with an anguished feeling in his chest. 'I have to go. Sean…'

'I heard.' She gave him a reassuring smile. 'Go. See Abigail. I'm going to be packing anyway. And… If we're both heading back to London, I can sort us some transport and a hotel at the other end?'

He blinked with surprise. 'You'd…really? Is that okay?'

'Gwyn, you've helped me through my crazy time the last few weeks. I'm hardly going to leave you alone to get through yours. And besides, I'm worried about Sean and Kayla too. London at seventeen with no contacts and no money? Not a great place to be.'

That was the thought that was eating him up inside too. That if he'd helped them, supported them right, they wouldn't have gone like this. They'd have trusted him and he could have kept them safe.

Another loved one he'd let down because he was distracted with his own stuff—in this case, Willow. He was running out of people to disappoint.

Still, he hesitated a moment. Letting Willow help meant letting Willow in even further. And she had enough on her own plate right now, anyway. But he did need to get to London…

'Thanks,' he said finally.

She gave him a weak smile and shooed him away with her hands. 'Then get going!'

'I will,' he said. 'As soon as I get my shirt back…'

It took surprisingly little time to repack her life.

Her heart, however, was struggling more than her head.

Mechanically, she placed all the things she'd brought with her from New York into Rowan's battered suitcase, since her sister had taken hers, realising belatedly how few of them she'd actually used. Life in Rumbelow called for a different aesthetic, but also a different mindset. She'd found herself drifting into her sister's clothes almost without noticing—and not just for the slightly more generous cut that Rowan preferred, which gave her expanding stomach more room to grow.

Other things, too, had changed. She'd barely used her hair styling tools since she'd arrived, embracing instead the slight natural wave to her hair that seemed more suited to the seaside. She'd read the books on Rowan's shelves rather than magazines—sinking into fiction rather than trying to keep up with the world she usually inhabited. She'd eaten more lasagne in the last few weeks than in the decade before.

And she'd laughed. She'd had fun. She'd relaxed. She'd felt…like herself.

And wasn't that what she'd come to Rumbelow for in the first place?

She sat on the bed and thought, for what seemed like a very long time. But actually, the answers she was looking for came more quickly than she could have imagined.

Then she picked up her phone and started to make arrangements.

Organising a private plane to fly them to the capital took a little finesse, but Willow knew people who knew people, so it wasn't too difficult. Securing a suite at her favourite London hotel was even easier. As was getting a table for dinner the following evening at the hottest new restaurant in town. Easier, in fact, than getting a table at the Star and Dragon for folk night because, here, nobody cared who she was. In London, they all wanted to impress— or at least get the publicity that her showing up for dinner at their restaurant would net them.

Last of all came the most difficult phone call. The one she really didn't want to make.

But she looked around her at Rowan's cottage, then moved to the window to watch the rolling waves for a moment, and glimpsed Gwyn's converted lifeboat station further around the cliffs, and knew it was time.

And so, drawing on everything she'd learned—about herself, about the future, the world, what she wanted from it, and the vision she had for her life—she pressed the screen and called.

He didn't answer right away, of course—that would have given her too much power. She counted the rings—*one, two, three, four, five*—and then…

'Hello, Ben. It's Willow.'

She waited until they were in the hotel suite she'd booked to tell Gwyn.

She'd meant to tell him before they left Rumbelow, but he was with his sister most of the night, and when he'd slipped between her sheets he'd needed her touch, not her words. Then they'd overslept, so the morning had been a scramble, getting them out to the private airfield in time for their flight.

Then she'd meant to tell him on the plane, but he was busy explaining how Abigail had managed to talk to Sean the night before and got an address from him of a friend they were crashing with, and the hope and tension on his face had told her this wasn't the time.

She'd thought about doing it in the car from the airport, but he'd sunk into a kind of melancholia she assumed was brought on by his memories of the city they were driving through, so she'd just held his hand and let him know she was there.

But now they were at the hotel, and she really couldn't put it off any longer. Unfortunately.

'I'm going to head straight out and see if I can find this place where they're staying.' Gwyn pulled a clean shirt from the suitcase he'd dumped on the sofa in the corner of the suite and tugged his own off. Willow watched, drinking in every last glimpse of him.

'Okay. I can't come with you, I'm afraid,' she said. 'I've...got an appointment of my own this evening.'

He turned to her in surprise, still barechested, one eyebrow raised. 'An appointment?'

Damn, she'd made it sound medical, and now he was worried. Although the truth wasn't all that much better, she supposed.

'I'm meeting Ben for dinner.' Just tug that

sticking plaster right off and hope the pain passes.

'You're…what?' He sounded more confused than angry, which made sense. Why would he be angry? She wasn't his…anything. And he had bigger problems than her ex to deal with, anyway.

'I didn't want him showing up in Rumbelow,' she explained. 'This way, I get to see him on my own terms.'

'You shouldn't have to see him at all!' Gwyn ran his hands through his hair, anguish on his face. 'I can't… I have to go find Sean. I can't come with you.' He looked so conflicted, so troubled by this that Willow almost laughed— except she was certain that would only make the situation worse.

'I wasn't asking you to,' she said lightly. Yes, she'd feel better with Gwyn by her side— somehow, she always did. But he wasn't going to be there after she went back to New York, and so she had to start getting used to doing things on her own again.

And she had to keep tamping down that tiny flame of hope that flickered on in her chest, that things could be different, somehow. The one that told her she wanted more than she was willing to admit, even to herself.

She'd forced Rowan into admitting her feelings for Eli. But she couldn't afford to do the same herself. She had to think about the future and the baby and Ben. And it wasn't fair to saddle Gwyn with any of that.

'You shouldn't go alone,' Gwyn said firmly. 'You said, when you came to Rumbelow, that you were afraid he'd steamroller over what you wanted, that he'd take control. You shouldn't see him alone. Wait until I've found Sean, then I can come with you.'

Willow shook her head. 'He wouldn't wait that long anyway. But honestly, it'll go better if I meet him alone. You don't need to worry.' She'd had plenty of time to think through exactly what she wanted to say. He wouldn't get the chance to steamroller her now.

She wasn't the same woman he'd known in New York, and she was kind of proud of that.

'But I do worry,' Gwyn replied, finally looking up to meet her gaze head-on. 'And that's a problem.'

'This is why I knew I should never have let myself get close to you.' Once again, the words tumbled out of Gwyn's mouth without him even meaning to say them—for all that they were true.

Willow blinked at him, eyes wide and her face paling. 'What do you mean?'

'The minute I let you in, that's when things started going wrong.' He was explaining himself badly, he knew, could tell from her hurt expression, but just because his choice of words was horrible didn't mean it wasn't the truth. 'I had things under control before then. Sean was safe, at home, listening to me. Abigail was happy. And that was all I needed. Then you showed up and I... I took my eye off the ball. I forgot that when I try to have more, care more, let more people in, things go wrong and people get hurt.' *People die.*

'Gwyn, if this is about Darrell...' Willow started, but he cut her off.

'Not just Darrell. Rachel. Even Abigail.' He'd never told her what had happened to his sister, he realised. He'd let her believe that she'd always been happy and healthy in Rumbelow. Never let on how hard they'd had to fight for that to be true.

'I never asked about Sean's dad,' Willow said slowly, carefully. She was quick, and clever. He'd liked that about her right from the start.

'He was an utter bastard,' Gwyn spat, the memories still raw after all these years. 'He got Abigail pregnant right after she finished her A-levels, and then they had to get married, of course.' There shouldn't have been any 'of course' about it, but that was how things were then, and there. But it had been a terrible idea, he'd known that from the start. He'd only been a teenager—and a young one—then. No one had listened to what he thought.

'He left?' Willow guessed.

'Not soon enough.' Abigail had never admitted how bad things were in her marriage. If he'd known, maybe he wouldn't have left for London—or maybe he would. 'I went to London when Sean was six and I think it was after that when things got really bad.' And maybe that wasn't because he'd gone, or maybe it was. All he knew was he hadn't been there to look after his sister when she'd needed him.

'What happened?'

Gwyn sat heavily on the bed and sighed. 'She never let on that there was a problem while I was gone. Not even when I visited. But when I came home after Darrell's death, four years later, I found her with a broken arm, Sean looking terrified and his dad gone. We've never seen him since.'

Abigail had thrown him out, he supposed.

And there were enough real men in the village to back her up and make sure she was safe.

But it should have been him.

Willow had her head tilted to the side, watching him.

'What?' he asked tetchily. He needed to get going, look for Sean. He couldn't let Abigail down again.

'I was just thinking that the last time you came to London you lost your girlfriend, an unborn baby, your best friend and bandmate *and* nearly lost your sister. No wonder you hate this place.'

'It's not the place I blame.'

'No. That much is clear.' She sat beside him on the edge of the bed, half on, half off, as if prepared to jump up again if he didn't want her there. But he *did* want her there—that was the problem. 'You know none of those things were your fault, right?'

She didn't understand.

'It doesn't matter. Maybe I could have stopped them, maybe I couldn't. The point is, I should have been there for the people I cared about. But they…there were too many of them. I couldn't be everywhere at once, and so I ended up letting them *all* down. That's why I have to keep it focused, concentrate on the only people I've got left—Abigail and Sean. It's why I can't afford to let anyone else in.'

'And why you don't want Sean in London,' she guessed. 'You're worried you won't be able to split your vigil between him here and Abigail in Rumbelow.'

He hadn't thought of it in those terms exactly, just known that if Sean came to London and got involved in the music scene, bad things might happen—like they had to Darrell. Oh, he knew his nephew was far more level-headed and less naive than his friend had been, not to mention that he had Kayla with him, who had to be a better guardian angel than Gwyn had managed to be for Darrell.

But none of that got rid of the heavy ball of fear that sat in his gut when he thought about Sean being here and Abigail being back in Cornwall, one of them always without his protection.

'It's not a vigil,' he snapped back. 'It's my family.'

'It's you martyring yourself, your whole *future,* to look after people who you think need you—but who would never want you to think this way,' she replied bluntly. 'All to make up for a series of events you couldn't have predicted or prevented wherever you were.'

He pulled away. 'You don't know what you're talking about.'

'Yes, I do,' she replied. 'Because I came to Rumbelow to hide this spring—I made no secret of that. But it means I know what hiding looks like. And while I hid out for a month or so while I figured things out, you've been hiding there for the last, what? Seven years? All because you're too scared to care for another person and risk losing them, or someone else getting hurt again.'

She said it like it was unreasonable.

'Why *shouldn't* I be there to look after my family? Isn't that what *matters* in this world?'

'Of course it is. But Gwyn, you have to ask yourself. Are you really looking after them? Are you giving them what they need—not what *you* need to feel safe? Because if you were, do you really think Sean would have run away to London without telling you first?'

Willow knew her words had hit home—hell, Gwyn practically flinched at them.

But then he shook them off, and hit back.

'What do you know about it? About family? I've been Rowan's neighbour for *years*, and I never even met you before. You came to Rumbelow because you needed help, not because you loved your family. If you did, you wouldn't have left her alone there.'

'She wanted to be alone.' It wasn't anything she hadn't thought herself before. She knew she'd been a bad sister—and she wanted to do better. But they weren't talking about her right now. 'Gwyn, I'm not saying you've done anything wrong. I'm saying that…people have to be responsible for themselves. You can love them, support them, but you can't save them from themselves in the end. You couldn't have saved Darrell, however hard you'd tried. Abigail…you weren't responsible for her marrying that man. And she wouldn't want you to be, you know that. She'd hate the idea that you were only staying in Rumbelow because you were worried about her and Sean. That you'd given up your career, your future, your *life* for them. You know she would.'

His shoulders deflated a little at that, and she knew she'd got her point home.

'It's not like I had anything else to live for anyway,' he said softly. 'I lost all that when Rachel miscarried and left. When Darrell…'

'I know.' She put a hand on his arm, trying to convey that she really was only trying to help. 'But you could have, couldn't you? You could have a new future.'

His gaze met hers and the agony she saw there tore into her chest.

'I can't risk it,' he said. 'I can't risk falling in love with you, Willow.'

And there it was. The word neither of them had been saying—the one she'd barely even let herself *think*.

Love.

Was it love when you just *knew* that the person standing before you was the one you wanted beside you whenever life got hard? Was it love when you just *looked* at a person and felt like maybe everything was going to be all right after all?

It was probably love when you couldn't imagine a future in which you weren't with them, wasn't it?

Oh, hell.

Gwyn might not be willing to risk it, but it was already too late for her.

She was in love with him. And he was about to walk out of the door.

'I have to go and find Sean. I'm sorry.' Gwyn paused by the door. 'Will you be here when I get back?'

'I don't know,' she answered honestly. Right now, it felt like she knew nothing at all—like everything was even less certain than the day she'd arrived in Rumbelow.

He nodded, as if he'd expected nothing less, then walked out of the door.

She let him go.

CHAPTER TWELVE

LONDON DIDN'T SEEM to have changed much in the seven years he'd been gone. Oh, the skyline might look a bit different in places, and the names on the storefronts might have updated, but it still *felt* the same.

It felt grimy and dangerous and like it wanted to suck him in.

He needed to get back to Cornwall. He needed to find Sean.

He *needed* to stop thinking about Willow.

The moment he'd told her he couldn't risk falling in love with her, he'd known it was a lie. He'd already fallen.

What he couldn't risk was letting her know. Giving her hope or expectations that he could be anything other than the man he was.

A broken, desperate man holding together the tatters of his old life with clutching hands.

He knew she was right. Abigail and Sean wouldn't want him to give up his dreams, his chance at love and happiness for them. But she didn't seem to realise how close he'd come to losing *everything* all at once. How terrified he'd been that it could all have been gone in an instant, if Abigail hadn't fought back that one time, that last time, the one time it mattered.

It was because of Sean, of course. He'd stood between his father and his mother, ready to take the beating instead. At ten, he'd thought he was ready to be the man of the house, Gwyn supposed.

Abigail hadn't let her husband touch him. And she'd suffered for it—but she'd also found the strength to make sure it never happened again. That was what mattered.

Gwyn had lived with them for the first six months he'd been home, when letting them out of his sight had been cause for a minor panic attack. They'd helped him find his way back to life, after losing Darrell and Rachel and the baby.

He owed them. He loved them. And keeping them safe was the most important thing in his life.

Which was why he was trawling the back streets of a rather less salubrious area of the capital, looking for his errant nephew and his girlfriend.

He found the place they were supposed to be staying easily enough, but of course they weren't there. The friend who'd let them couch surf there the last couple of nights directed him towards a bar a few Tube stops away, where they were apparently playing that night— and possibly now rooming at, by the sound of things.

Wearily, Gwyn hoisted his backpack onto his shoulders again and went to find it.

He could have left his bag at the hotel. Should have, maybe. But he hadn't known, when he'd left, if he'd be going back. Still didn't, if he was honest. Besides, the bag wasn't *that* heavy. It only held his essentials for a night or two. Not like Willow's bulging suitcase, ready for her return to New York.

She might even be gone by now; she hadn't told him the time of her flight, or if she had he'd not been paying enough attention to retain the information.

But no, she couldn't fly out yet. Because Ben was flying *in,* just to speak to her.

Would what had passed between them in the hotel room that afternoon change how Willow dealt with her ex? Would knowing that he'd written off any chance of a future between them make her more likely to go back to Ben?

She'd said from the start that wasn't what she wanted. But she might not want to raise the baby alone either…

He swallowed down the bile that rose in his throat at the thought of Willow and Ben together. Of that man he'd never met worming his way back into Willow's life, and making her life a misery. Worse, treating his child badly. Willow hadn't said a huge amount about Ben's behaviour and he had no reason to believe he'd ever physically hurt her, but there were other forms of abuse too. He couldn't let anything happen to her.

But how would he stop it? She'd be in New York, Abigail would be in Rumbelow and Sean… Sean would apparently be here, at the Black Crow Club, performing for drunk Londoners or tourists who didn't appreciate him.

He sighed as he looked up at the looming black bird on the sign out front, even the image a horrible reminder of his past, then pushed open the door.

It was early enough in the evening that the place was still mostly deserted; this was the kind of club that came to life in the early hours, the dead of night. Gwyn remembered places like this. It was exactly the sort of place he and Darrell would have played, back in the day.

The man behind the bar looked up with faint interest as he walked in.

'I'm looking for Sean Callaghan.'

'Wait, aren't you Gwyn...whatsisname? Used to be in that band, Blackbird? Whatever happened to you guys?' The barman looked far more interested now, just not in what Gwyn wanted him to care about.

'I'm Sean Callaghan's uncle and I'm here to take him home,' he said, more firmly. 'Where is he?'

'Uncle Gwyn?' Sean emerged from a back room, guitar slung over his back. 'What are you doing here?'

The barman, clearly sensing that he wasn't needed for this discussion, and probably didn't want to be part of it anyway, slunk off to the other end of the bar.

'I'm here to take you home,' Gwyn said. He was done with this. People just needed to do what was best to keep themselves safe, so he could sleep at night.

Kayla appeared behind Sean, looking defiant. 'We're playing a gig here tonight. We're not going anywhere.'

'You're seventeen,' Gwyn replied baldly. 'Neither of you should even *be* in here.'

'Uncle Gwyn...' Sean placed his guitar down

on the nearest table and, leaving Kayla to guard it, approached him gingerly. He spoke softly, but reasonably—like an adult, Gwyn realised. He'd never thought of Sean as an adult before. 'I know you have good reasons to be afraid of me being part of the music scene here. And I know you're only here because you care about me and you want me to be safe. I talked about this a lot with Mum before I left. But the thing is, this is my future. This is the life I want to experience. And I'd really hope you could support me in that.'

Gwyn wondered if Sean had been practising that speech in the mirror. It was good—reasoned and reasonable, calmly delivered.

And it didn't make a damn bit of difference in the face of his own fears. Maybe, he realised, because *they* weren't rational at all. Because even *knowing* that didn't stop the rising acid that burned his throat, or the heat that flushed through him, or the way his hands flexed as if he wanted to *drag* Sean to safety.

He forced himself to keep his voice even, like Sean's. 'I know you think you're an adult, that you can face the world alone, but you don't know anything about this world.'

'Because you'd never tell me!' Sean shot back, some of his composure fading now. 'My whole life I've been asking you about music, about your career, and you'd never talk about any of it. And I get it, I do—what happened to you and Darrell was awful. But it's like you want to pretend that he never existed!'

Did he? Maybe. It was easier that way. But he wasn't going to admit that to Sean.

'My past isn't a story for your entertainment, Sean.'

'That's not—you *know* that's not what I meant!' Exasperated, Sean ran a hand through his hair. Kayla came to stand beside him, one hand on his arm, but stayed silent. When he spoke again, Sean sounded calmer, as if her touch alone had grounded him.

Gwyn knew how that felt. Willow had done that for him too.

'You know my dreams, Uncle Gwyn. You've known almost as long as I have that this is the life I wanted. And you...you know and understand this world better than anyone! I want you on my side for it, I want to do this *with* you, not against you. But I need you to trust me. And I have to do it, however that looks. I can't live my life in the shadow of *your* fear.'

Reality smashed over Gwyn like a soundwave, like that first crashing chord on the guitar before the song started.

'I can't live my life in the shadow of your fear.'

Wasn't that what he was asking everyone to do? Abigail had barely dated since her husband left and he knew at least part of that was because she knew how many questions he'd ask, how he'd hover and worry. Sean had run away to London not because Gwyn wouldn't help him, but because he was actively trying to stop him seeking his dream.

And Willow...

Willow was facing down her ex alone because he was too scared to let himself love her.

All this fear, all this trying to keep everyone safe, it had only driven them further away—and into danger.

And it was tearing him apart.

How had he not seen it?

Sean deflated a little, the longer Gwyn stayed silent.

'Look, just stay for the show tonight, yeah? See what you think. I know you've seen us play back home but it's different here, right? Stay, and listen. See if you think we've got what it takes. And if you do...'

Gwyn swallowed, and forced himself to speak. 'I'll support you. Because you're right. I... If you want to do this, I... I'd rather you do it with me than without me.'

Maybe he couldn't keep everybody he loved safe. Maybe he had to let them make their own mistakes.

But that didn't mean he couldn't support them. Cheer them on. And be there when— no, not when, *if*—if things went wrong.

He'd do that for Sean. For Abigail.

And maybe he'd even get to do it for Willow, when she was ready.

Willow chose her outfit for dinner with Ben carefully.

Attractive but not too sexy. Confident but not obnoxiously intimidating. Cut so that her stomach wouldn't strain against the fabric. Heels she could walk easily in. Hair up, and lipstick on.

It wasn't a battle. But it was a negotiation. Even if he didn't know it yet.

He was already sitting at the table she'd booked in the restaurant when she arrived. A classic power-play. He'd sat with his back to the wall so he could watch her approaching. In meetings, she knew, he liked to arrive last to show that he was the one in control. Here, though, he was probably hoping to put her on the back foot by making her feel she needed to apologise for being late, even though she wasn't.

She did not apologise.

He stood to greet her and she froze as he reached out to kiss her cheek in welcome. Pulling away, she dropped into the seat opposite him.

'Ben. Thank you for coming.' He'd already ordered wine for them, she realised, but obviously she wouldn't be drinking that. She flagged down a passing waiter and asked for a lime and soda.

'Well, when your girlfriend drops off the planet and hires an impersonator to take her place, you kind of want to find out why,' he drawled.

She didn't point out that Rowan wasn't an impersonator, she was her twin, and that she hadn't exactly hired her. That was what he wanted—her on the defensive, arguing the smaller points so she forgot about the bigger ones.

Not this time.

'I came home to England because I needed time to think.' She folded her hands over the menu. 'Rowan needed an adventure, so I sent her to house-sit my apartment. It worked out for both of us.'

'Since she seduced my brother and sent him to take over my company, I'm guessing it worked out best for her,' Ben replied, bitterness colouring his voice.

Rowan was already on her way back to the UK—might even have already landed—Willow knew. And from the last phone call they'd shared, Willow wasn't sure things were working out at all for her twin.

Of course, they weren't working out for her yet either.

'So, are you done thinking?' Ben asked. 'Are you coming home?'

Home. He meant New York, she supposed. He meant home to *him* too.

'Ben, I didn't ask you here so we could get back together,' she said firmly. 'That's never going to happen.'

'Why the hell not?' He banged his wine glass down on the table. 'We had a good thing going, you and me, until you ran away here and screwed me over. Everything was fine until you left!'

'Everything was not fine.' She knew that now. When she'd been in it, her relationship with Ben had seemed…functional, at least. Maybe the best she'd thought she could hope for, or deserved. After all, she had beauty, money, fame, success. Surely she couldn't ask for more—couldn't ask for someone to look past those things and love her for who she really was, not what she could give them?

But then she'd come to Rumbelow and met Gwyn. And suddenly, she'd known it *was* possible—even if he wouldn't admit it. She loved him, and she was pretty sure he loved her too—or could, if he'd let himself.

And if he never did… Well, she knew what it felt like now, being truly loved. And she wasn't going to settle for anything less. She wanted a life and a love that lit her up—not just for herself, but for her baby too.

'Ben, what we had wasn't a real relationship—it was a business arrangement.'

'One that worked very well for both of us,' he interjected.

'Well, it's not working for me any more.' She took a breath. 'Ben, I'm pregnant.'

If she'd had any doubt about whether she was doing the right thing, deciding to raise this baby apart from its father, the look of horror that melted into disgust on Ben's face ended it.

'God, why? Are you going to get rid of it?' Ben asked. 'Wait, it's not *mine*, is it?'

'Biologically? Yes. Practically…it doesn't have to be,' she said. 'I'm going to be raising this child. If you want to be involved in their life, we can talk about what that might look like. If you don't… I'm not going to ask for anything from you.'

'Wait, wait. If it *is* mine, we should get married, right? That's the heir to the company in there. Pending a DNA test, of course.' She could see the calculations going on behind his eyes now—what a child, or at least an heir, could mean. He'd said something about his brother taking over the company. She'd always known that a large part of her value to him was making him look like a stable, responsible family man just waiting for that ring and the family to happen. Maybe he was thinking this was his way to regain that reliable standing in the eyes of the world—or at least the board of directors.

Time to shoot down that idea.

'No, Ben. It's a baby. Not the heir to anything—just its own person. It doesn't need your money, or the pressure of living up to your ideals or expectations. It just needs to be itself.' She frowned. 'And we are absolutely *not* getting married.'

'Then the kid will be a bastard. Illegitimate.' He spat it as if that was the worst thing that could happen to a child.

Willow could think of far worse.

'They'll be loved,' she countered.

Ben shook his head. 'I need to think about this.'

That was fair. She'd taken her time. He deserved some too.

She pushed her chair back from the table. She wasn't hungry any more, anyway.

'Take all the time you need,' she said. 'You know how to find me when you're ready.'

'No.' He grabbed her arm and yanked it until she had no choice but to sit back down. 'You want me to work with you on this, to find a fair way to deal with the situation?'

'It's not a situation, it's a child,' she replied. 'But yes. I'd like it if we could discuss it like adults and come to a mutually agreeable way forward.' That wasn't so much to ask, was it?

From Ben's steely expression, it seemed that it was—or at least, that he was going to demand a steep price for it.

'You want me to work *with* you on this, and not call up my lawyer right now and set him on the case, you need to come back to New York with me. Tonight.'

CHAPTER THIRTEEN

WILLOW WASN'T IN the hotel room when he got back from the club in the early hours of the next morning—not that he'd really expected her to be.

A quick call to the receptionist confirmed that she'd checked out hours ago, while he'd been watching Sean and Kayla perform, and realigning his world view to include the fact that his nephew was potentially going to be the star he'd never quite managed to be, and that this was a *good* thing.

That wasn't the only realigning of reality he'd been mentally performing either, but without Willow there to hear it the rest seemed meaningless right now.

'She didn't leave a message for me?' he asked the receptionist, trying not to sound too desperate. But his own phone was silent, devoid of contact. Surely she wouldn't have left for New York without telling him?

Except she *had* told him. And he'd told her that he could never love her. So why on earth did he think she would stay?

'No message,' the receptionist replied pityingly.

'Right.' Gwyn hung up.

After a restless, unsettled night, he met Sean and Kayla for brunch and, between them, they hammered out a plan for getting them known, signed and famous—the right way. Gwyn held himself back from adding too many safety checks to the plan, but it was clear he was going to be spending a lot of time in London with them, if only for his own peace of mind.

'You realise at this point you're basically our manager,' Sean said, between mouthfuls of bacon.

Gwyn ignored him and carried on setting out the plan. One step at a time.

After brunch, and after setting them up in an acceptable short-term rental for the next couple of weeks, with strict instructions about their next moves, Gwyn headed for the station, and back to Cornwall.

Everything inside him was itching to race straight to the airport and grab the next flight to New York, but he made himself wait. He needed to report back to Abigail. Grab more things than just his overnight bag—and make sure that Sean and Kayla were okay in London alone, before he disappeared off across the ocean.

More than that, he needed to give Willow the time and space to do what *she* needed to do, before he barrelled into her life again with any dramatic declarations.

Which didn't mean he wasn't practising those declarations in his head, in preparation.

I'm an idiot. I love you. Of course I love you, and I can't believe I ever thought I could stop it. I want to spend the rest of my life with you and the baby. And yes, I'm still terrified, but it's going to be worth it. I'm sure of it.

When he wasn't imagining those conversations, however, darker thoughts and possibilities filled his mind.

Ones where Willow announced she was marrying Ben. Or that she never wanted to set foot in Rumbelow—or see him—again. Worse, ones where her plane crashed, or her taxi from the airport caused a pile-up, and he wasn't there to save her. Not that he knew quite what he'd do in the event of a plane crash, but still. The feelings lingered.

He shook them away and focused on everything he'd say when he got to New York and found her.

He was still planning the conversation in his head when he walked up the cliff road towards the old lifeboat station he called home, and past Rowan's cottage—and saw a willowy blonde standing in the garden.

His heart jumped in his chest, everything suddenly feeling tight and light at the same time. She raised a hand and waved and—

He realised the truth. It was Rowan. He could tell the difference now, even at this distance. And what that said about how far gone he was for Willow he didn't want to know.

He called out a greeting, and she gave him a sad smile in return. He wasn't sure exactly what had gone on with her in New York, but he was pretty sure she hadn't found her happy ending either.

Yet.

He still had hopes that his would be waiting at the other end of a transatlantic flight, if he could get the words right. It was like songwriting. Sometimes it could take a hundred drafts to find exactly the right words, ordered the right way, to say what he was trying to say.

When he had the words right, he'd go to New York.

He opened the door to his house and stepped inside, the glorious view out over the sea not captivating him for once. He was too lost in thought.

Until a voice said, 'Hello, Gwyn.'

He spun round to find her leaning against the kitchen counter. The small swell of her belly seemed to have increased overnight, emphasised, perhaps, by the loose shirt she had knotted over her jeans—one of his, he suspected.

In the rush of relief and joy at seeing her, all his carefully planned words flew from his head.

'What are you doing here? Not that I'm… I thought you'd be back in New York already.'

'That's what Ben wanted,' she replied. 'Gave me an ultimatum and everything. Fly back to New York with him or he'd make things difficult for me with the baby.'

'And you…'

'Called his bluff.' Willow gave a light shrug, a small smile on her lips. 'He wants me there to prove he's a responsible, reliable family man. An ugly custody battle or financial wrangling doesn't do that for him. He needs me a hell of a lot more than I need him, so I'll go back when I'm good and ready. I had unfinished business here.'

With him, he assumed. 'Why didn't you wait for me at the hotel?' Gwyn asked.

'Rowan called. She'd just arrived at Heathrow and…well, she needed me. I didn't know how long you'd need to be in London. So I got us a car and we travelled back here together. And she happens to have your spare key in case of emergencies, doesn't she? So I figured I'd just wait for you here.'

Thank God she had. Now, if he could just remember everything he had planned to say to her…

Willow took a deep breath. It was almost the moment of truth. The moment when she figured out what happened next—and if, just maybe, she could have everything she wanted.

But first… 'Did you find Sean? Are he and Kayla okay?'

'They're just fine,' he assured her. 'Far more mature and capable than I was at that age. And I think…with my support and guidance, they're going to be amazing.'

With his support. He was putting himself back out there at last—acting in the pursuit of dreams rather than hiding from them in fear of everything that could go wrong.

Maybe that meant he'd be able to do the same with her.

She opened her mouth to find out, but Gwyn beat her to it.

'I've been an idiot,' he said.

She looked up at him, studying his face for answers. 'You think you've been an idiot?' Hope started to float in her chest.

'Yes. I should have told you weeks ago that I was falling in love with you. I should have told you yesterday that I love you—and your baby—more than anything else in this world. That, if you'll have me, I want to spend every day of the rest of my life making you happy.' Not keeping them safe, she noted—although she was sure he'd want that too. But perhaps he understood a little better now that there was a fine line between keeping someone safe and limiting them—and himself.

Wait. Willow blinked, and focused in on the really important part of his statement. 'You love me? Us?'

'More than anything,' he repeated and stepped closer, opening his arms to let her in.

She moved into them without hesitation, resting her head against his chest. 'Even though I'm pregnant with another man's child?'

'Did you not hear me say I love the baby too?'

'And even though people will be watching and gossiping about us? Even though they'll dredge up every awful story they can about either of us? Especially if Ben gets involved.'

'You know, I thought I was the one finding reasons this couldn't work,' he pointed out. 'I doubt you can think of any I haven't already thought of. And I don't care. You matter more to me than any of that.'

She looked up and met his gaze. 'Even if I want to go back to New York?'

That was the big one, wasn't it? Was he ready or willing to stop hiding away in Rumbelow and face the real world again?

She really hoped so.

'Then I'll come with you,' he replied. 'As long as we can come back to Rumbelow often. I'd miss my sea view.'

'So would I,' Willow replied, looking down at her bump to hide the tears she could feel pricking behind her eyes. Tears of happiness, of relief and of sheer amazement. 'And my sister. This baby is going to need all the aunts and uncles it can get.'

'I think it's going to have plenty,' Gwyn assured her. 'Abigail is going to be over the moon, for one.'

Willow hummed her agreement, then caught

his gaze again. She needed to ask, even though it terrified her. 'You're sure about this? I mean, just yesterday afternoon, you said—'

'I know what I said.' And he didn't much want to relive it, by the sound of things. 'But you were right. And so was Sean. I was so scared... I was living a half-life. And I was forcing everyone else to just exist in it with me. It wasn't fair on them, on you—or on me. And it's not what I want any more.' He rested his forehead against hers. 'I'm lucky enough to still be here when Darrell isn't. I owe it to him to keep living for both of us. And if I only have this one life to live—I want to live it to the full, by being madly, passionately, irrevocably in love with you.'

'I can live with that.' A wide smile broke out across Willow's face, so wide it made her cheeks hurt. 'Did I mention I love you too?'

'You didn't,' he said, sounding amused. 'But I was hoping.'

'I do. I love you, and this baby is going to love you, and neither of us are going to have to hide from that, or any of our dreams, ever again.' Not if she had anything to do with it, anyway.

'I'm glad,' Gwyn replied. 'I'm tired of hiding. I'm ready to live again—with you.' And then he kissed her. Something she hoped he'd be doing over and over again for as long as they both drew breath.

EPILOGUE

FOLK NIGHT AT the Star and Dragon was always a big deal, but tonight it was bigger than ever. Local lights, Sean and Kayla, were back from a very successful few months in London, where they were definitely getting noticed—as Gwyn had been proudly telling anyone who'd listen—and were performing on home turf again.

Willow settled back into her seat, her over-sized belly filling all the space between her chair and the plate of lasagne in front of her.

'That baby better come soon, Will,' her sister Rowan joked. 'Or you won't be able to reach your lasagne.'

'And that would be a travesty,' Rowan's fiancé Eli said, as he polished off his own plateful. 'This stuff is amazing. How can a tiny Cornish village have better lasagne than New York City?'

'Rumbelow is a pretty special place,' Willow replied. 'Look at what it's done for all of us.'

She'd gone back to New York at first, but it had been lonely without Gwyn, who'd stayed in the UK to help Sean and Kayla get settled in London. More than that, she just didn't feel like the same woman who'd fled the city in a panic, pregnant and alone and scared. She'd changed. Rumbelow—and, more importantly, Gwyn—had changed her.

By the time Ben had decided once and for all that he didn't want to be involved in the baby's life, she'd already come to the conclusion that, for the next little while at least, New York wasn't where she belonged.

She'd travelled back to Rumbelow before her doctors told her not to fly any more. She figured her plane must have passed Rowan's in mid-air, as her sister flew back to be in the city with her fiancé. They visited often though, splitting their time between America and the UK. Eventually, Willow hoped she and Gwyn would be able to do the same.

Up on the stage, Sean and Kayla finished their last song, to rapturous applause. Sean stepped up to the microphone and spoke over the clapping. 'That's it from us for now. But if you ask him nicely, I think Uncle Gwyn has a new song he'd like to play tonight.'

Willow looked at her boyfriend curiously.

She'd heard him tinkering around with some new chords and melodies recently, but he hadn't said anything about a new song. But as the crowd called out, he grabbed his guitar and headed for the stage.

'Do you know anything about this?' Willow asked Abigail, sitting beside her.

Gwyn's sister just smiled.

The pub fell silent as Gwyn started to play— a tune beautiful and somehow full of hope. But it was the words that really caught at her heart.

They wouldn't mean anything to anyone else, she was sure. It probably sounded like a generic folk song. But under them, she heard everything that mattered.

He sang about fear. About hiding from love. About opening his arms to let someone in. About how life rarely gave him what he wanted, and how every knock and blow pushed him down, away from what he was meant to have.

But he also sang about how, when the moment was right, the perfect person could pull him back up.

Could help him face the world again.

And he sang about how he'd never let that person go.

Willow bit her lip as the song came to an

end, and the audience went wild. But the show wasn't over just yet.

'So, how about it, Willow?' Gwyn asked into the microphone, the words echoing in the suddenly silent pub. Because he was down on one knee, a ring box in his hand. 'Want to spend the rest of our lives together officially? You, me and our baby?'

Willow felt the whole world shift into focus, exactly the way it had always meant to be, and smiled.

'Yes,' she replied. 'Starting right now.'

* * * * *

*If you missed the previous story in
the Twin Sister Swap duet
then check out*

Cinderella in the Spotlight

*And if you enjoyed this story
check out these other great reads
from Sophie Pembroke*

Best Man with Benefits
Baby Surprise in Costa Rica
Their Icelandic Marriage Reunion

All available now!